Edge heard the f....................................or of the restaurant..................................d-way down his arr....................................li-ness. He whirled, ...at but managing only to draw his left arm free of a sleeve. As he turned, he glimpsed the face of Billings, which showed a mixture of shock, rage, and fear. Then he saw Ramon, the Mexican, pressed against the rear wall to one side of the bead-curtained archway, terrified to a point close to passing out. Finally, the prematurely bald man with the scar on his jaw who had emanated so much ill-will toward the half-breed last night. Now his eyes were no longer brooding; instead they blazed with green fire to complement the way his lips were drawn back from his teeth in a vicious snarl. The sun-glinting blade of the knife in his right hand was just three feet away from Edge's chest as the half-breed completed his awkward turn.

"Grogan!" Billings roared.

Edge swung his right arm forward, to whiplash his coat toward the thrusting knife. Grogan pulled up short and vented an obscenity as he tried to jerk the knife clear. He did so, but lost time. Enough time for Edge to streak his left hand into the long hair at the nape of his neck and slide out the straight razor.

"He's on his own, Edge!" Billings shrieked.

"Not for long," the half-breed hissed between teeth clenched in a killer's grin. . . .

WARNING

*This story is not for
the faint-hearted reader.*

THE EDGE SERIES:

#1 THE LONER
#2 TEN GRAND
#3 APACHE DEATH
#4 KILLER'S BREED
#5 BLOOD ON SILVER
#6 RED RIVER
#7 CALIFORNIA KILL
#8 HELL'S SEVEN
#9 BLOODY SUMMER
#10 BLACK VENGEANCE
#11 SIOUX UPRISING
#12 DEATH'S BOUNTY
#13 THE HATED
#14 TIGER'S GOLD
#15 PARADISE LOSES
#16 THE FINAL SHOT
#17 VENGEANCE VALLEY
#18 TEN TOMBSTONES
#19 ASHES AND DUST
#20 SULLIVAN'S LAW
#21 RHAPSODY IN RED
#22 SLAUGHTER ROAD
#23 ECHOES OF WAR
#24 SLAUGHTERDAY
#25 VIOLENCE TRAIL
#26 SAVAGE DAWN
#27 DEATH DRIVE
#28 EVE OF EVIL
#29 THE LIVING, THE DYING, AND THE DEAD
#30 TOWERING NIGHTMARE
#31 THE GUILTY ONES
#32 THE FRIGHTENED GUN

WRITE FOR OUR FREE CATALOG

If there is a Pinnacle Book you want—and you cannot find it locally—it is available from us simply by sending the title and price plus 50¢ per order and 10¢ per copy to cover mailing and handling costs to:

Pinnacle Book Services
P.O. Box 690
New York, N.Y. 10019

Please allow 4 weeks for delivery. New York State and California residents add applicable sales tax.

——Check here if you want to receive our catalog regularly.

Best-Selling Series!

#**32** The Most Violent
Westerns in Print

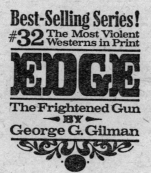

EDGE

The Frightened Gun

BY

George G. Gilman

PINNACLE BOOKS   •   LOS ANGELES

This is a work of fiction. All the characters and
events portrayed in this book are fictional, and any
resemblance to real people or incidents is purely
coincidental.

EDGE #32: THE FRIGHTENED GUN

Copyright © 1979 by George G. Gilman

All rights reserved, including the right to reproduce
this book or portions thereof in any form.

First American edition.
First published in Great Britain by New English
Library, Limited, 1979.

A Pinnacle Books edition, published by special
arrangement with New English Library, London.

First printing, December 1979

ISBN: 0-523-40533-2

Cover illustration by Bruce Minney

Printed in the United States of America

PINNACLE BOOKS, INC.
2029 Century Park East
Los Angeles, California 90067

For E.R.C., who came through
with essential supplies on a very wet day.

THE FRIGHTENED GUN

Chapter One

A HOT wind had been blowing down out of the Sierras all morning and the man riding south across the Sarcobatus Flats toward the California state line was as gray as the mare under him, with the dust which the mountain wind stirred up and pasted to his sweating face and lodged in the fibers of his clothing.

Then, at midday, the air became still; hotter than it had ever been, but at least the man and his mount could open their mouths without feeling the searing bite of grit against their throats. For a while the horizon was veiled by curtains of moving dust clouds but soon these were swept aside and the vastness of the dry, baked-hard country could be seen to the full extent of the far distant encircling sandstone and limestone mountain ranges. With, here and there on the flats, an occasional clump of brush, a scattering of saguaro, cholla and prickly pear and—beyond the fringes of the flats—groups of low mesas and buttes.

As he reined in the mare, unhooked one of the canteens from the saddlehorn and took a small drink of tepid water, the man looked in every direction; carefully and without haste, checking that he was alone and that he had not veered off his chosen course during the dust storm. Then, his mind and thirst satisfied, he swung down to the ground, poured a little water in his sweat-smelling hat and allowed the horse to drink. This done, he beat the hat against his thigh a few times, dusted off his clothes with his hands, used his kerchief to wipe the sweat and dirt from his face and remounted to continue his ride

1

southward. As slowly as before. Almost as slowly, it seemed, as the sun moved along its afternoon course toward the far-off ridges in the west.

The horse had no name the man knew of. The man had for many years been called Edge.

He was tall and deceptively lean-looking, with not an ounce of excess flesh on his rangy frame which tipped the scales close to two hundred pounds. He was dressed in somber hues—the low-crowned and wide-brimmed hat was gray, as was his cotton shirt and the kerchief which was loosely knotted at the front; his denim pants and spurless riding boots were black. There was a brown leather gunbelt around his waist with a standard Remington revolver in the holster tied down to his right thigh. Even the colored wooden beads on the thong around his neck had faded to lusterless imitations of the bright shades they once had been.

All his clothing was scuffed and worn, stained and torn, badly repaired or not repaired at all. Long used, also, was the Western saddle and its accoutrements—the Winchester jutting from the forward canting boot on the right side as impersonal and lacking in fancy refinements as the revolver in the holster.

Thus, from the broad shoulders down he looked like any one of a thousand or more lone riders who might this day be drifting across the seemingly limitless parched country of the American Southwest. With or without a specific destination in mind. Leaving a job or looking for one. Recalling the past or reviewing the future. But, for the most part, uncaring because here in the present there was a fit horse to ride and supplies enough in the saddlebags to provide for immediate needs.

But, of course, above the shoulders was what made every drifter—every man—different from all the others. In the set of his features and in the mysterious darkness of the inside of his head.

The man called Edge had the kind of face which

2

could be regarded as either handsome or ugly. It did not matter what expression he wore, it depended upon how the beholder responded to the unmistakable signs in it of latent cruelty. In the eyes mostly, which were the lightest of blue and permanently narrowed under hooded lids. Eyes which looked as cold as slivers of ice but much harder. Also in the thinness and length of the lips. But sometimes the lips would part, drawing back from the evenly matched white teeth to display a smile. And sometimes there would be warmth in the smile. Never, though, did this expression melt the chill from the eyes.

Beneath the mouth his jawline was firm, the skin drawn taut from the high cheekbones which flanked a rather hawk-like nose. This skin was stained to the color of his gunbelt and saddle by more than just continual exposure to the elements, and was engraved with deep-cut lines which were not caused solely by the passing of close to forty years. For he had always been dark-skinned, this coloration deriving from the Mexican blood-line of his father—just as the ice-blueness of his eyes was inherited from his Scandinavian mother, while many of the cracks in his skin had been caused by the physical suffering and mental anguish he had endured during more recent years.

A morning's bristles grew on his cheeks, jaw and neck as he rode south through the furnace heat of the afternoon, more thickly along his top lip and down toward his jaw at either side of his mouth to indicate a bandito-type moustache. Black, like the thick hair which he wore long enough to brush his shoulders at either side and conceal the collar of his shirt at the back; this because he preferred to wear his hair long, rather than to cover the handle of a straight razor which jutted at the nape of his neck from a pouch held in place by the beaded thong.

As he rode south at an easy pace that conserved his own energy and that of the horse, his sweat-sheened features were in repose and impassive, revealing no visible sign of any discomfort or weariness. Which did not, of course, make him unique. For any man who chose the life of a drifting loner— or had it thrust upon him—soon learned to accept without complaint the worst with which the country and its elements could assault him. For if a man did not experience the worst, how was he to appreciate the best?

But what did make the man called Edge different from most—whatever their mode of living—was the way he remained constantly alert and always poised to respond should his ever-watching eyes see a sign of potential danger.

His vigilance was obvious, to the close observer, from the way his eyes moved in their sockets and from the number of times he cast backward glances over either shoulder. But far more subtle was the way he held the reins, the manner in which his feet rested in the stirrups and how he sat astride the saddle; isolated clues to the fact that this man, while appearing to be totally at ease on the vast and apparently deserted stretch of terrain, was prepared to react instantly should the need arise. And, if the clue to his latent cruel streak were also seen, the perceptive observer would guess that the reaction was likely to be a harsh one.

But for most of the scorchingly hot afternoon the slow riding half-breed saw nothing to give him even pause for thought. However, he never relaxed his vigilance for a moment, maintaining it with effortless ease. Without having to think about it—in the same manner as he took out the makings of a cigarette from time to time, rolled the tobacco in the paper, lit it and smoked it. Both sets of actions were habits which had been developed over many years. One a self-indulgent luxury. The other an often-proved necessity in staying alive.

The day was aging toward evening and the low sun was casting his shadow long across the arid ground to his left when he saw a patch of white

4

smoke smudge the dark blue sky directly ahead of him. He took mental note of this new element of his surroundings and continued to scan the country in every direction as he maintained the unhurried walking pace toward the eastern end of the low mesa above which the smoke hung.

He was perhaps a mile and a half away from the mesa when he first saw the sign of a fire, riding along the side of a rock-littered arroyo that cut a broad, shallow curve across the flats and went from sight beyond the forty-feet-high sandstone formation. Fifteen minutes later, when he was close enough to smell the burning brush, the smoke was rising as an uninterrupted column.

To the south of the mesa the curve of the dry wash sharpened to cut down the steepest strip of a shallow drop into a wide hollow in the lee of the sandstone escarpment. It was at the bottom of this hollow that the fire burned. Small and controlled—the cooking fire of a camp. Out of sight of Edge who had halted the mare on the lip of the hollow; for there was a dense growth of mesquite and juniper which obscured his view—except where the waters of infrequent flash storms had rushed down to carve a course through the brush and timber. On the downgrade the wash was much narrower and deeper than out on the flats north of the mesa. Smoothly and silently, the half-breed slid from his saddle and led the horse down to the timber, where he hitched the reins around a juniper branch.

He could now smell the appetizing aroma of coffee grounds boiling in a pot as well as wood smoke. And he could hear the crackle of brushwood attacked by flames. So he stepped very carefully down into the dry wash and watched where he was putting his feet so that he did not set any of the bed rocks skittering along the water course.

The mesa was formed in a curved shape, like half a horseshoe around the north and west rims of the hollow, so that the ground below was in deep evening shadow. The hungry flames sent constantly moving tongues of firelight through the darkening dusk. When, therefore, Edge reached the lower fringe of the twenty-feet-wide band of timber, he was able to see the component parts of the campsite quite distinctly.

The cooking fire with a coffee pot standing in the flames was some fifty feet from where he stood, and twenty feet back from the bank of the dry wash. Beyond this, a city-style delivery wagon was parked, the two-horse team still in the traces. Beside the fire, his back to where the half-breed stood watching, a man sat, cross-legged and with shoulders hunched—in an attitude which suggested that as he gazed into the heart of the flames, his expression would be morose. A short-of-stature, slight-of-build man wearing a black frock coat and a gray, Montana-peak cowhand's hat. The hat fit him well enough but looked incongruous on such a short, thin man and in combination with the coat.

Having seen this much—that the man was alone and the least likely source of trouble he had come across on his long ride out of the Middle-West— Edge opened his mouth to speak and prepared to step up from the dry wash. But kept his brown-skinned right hand close to the jutting butt of the holstered Remington, aware that his first impression could be proved wrong.

"One," the man at the fire said, hissing the word through clenched teeth as he straightened his back and raised his shoulders.

Edge held still and remained silent, his forehead creasing in a frown of perplexity.

"Two . . . three!" the man added quickly.

Then unfolded his arms, powered into a turn, drew a revolver from a holster at the center of his belt, hurled himself full length across the dusty ground and blasted a shot toward the half-breed.

Instead of an even-voiced call of greeting, a rasping curse escaped from Edge's partly opened mouth

6

as he dived to the bed of the dry wash. And he followed it with a more forceful obscenity as he felt the pain of impact against dozens of misshapen rocks which dug into him from knees to chest. But fear of dying from a stranger's bullet together with ice-cold anger at the man behind the gun transcended the jarring effect on his nervous system. So that the Remington, hammer cocked, remained firmly held in his right fist as he pushed himself up onto all fours, taking care to ensure that the line of his back stayed below the level of the arroyo bank.

"Oh, sweet Jesus!" the man at the fire shrieked, the first word in unison with the thud of the revolver bullet into a juniper trunk. "Dear God in heaven! Oh, I'm sorry! I didn't mean to . . . I was just tryin' to hit the . . . Please, mister, it wasn't supposed to be aimed at . . ."

Edge had long ago learned to control his fear and anger in life or death situations. And he was clear headed, all his senses totally receptive as he started to rise. So that he heard the man's words distinctly and was able to recognize the dread which caused his voice to quaver. Thus, as he came erect, his movements were slow and although his finger was tight against the trigger of the Remington, he was able without any mental effort to prevent it from squeezing the final fraction of an inch.

The man by the fire was still on the ground. But he had turned himself around so that he was entirely face forward toward the stranger he had almost killed—but he was lying awkwardly for both his arms were thrust into the air, the hands empty.

Despite his self-control, Edge could feel that his lips were still curled back and his skin was stretched tauter than ever to display the cold-eyed killer grin that had been the last human expression many men had seen. In the moving light of the fire's flames the look was perhaps more terrifying than in other circumstances. Certainly it caused the final vestiges of color to drain from the man's face, pulled his eyes to

7

their widest extent and constricted his throat so that the single-word plea which he was able to voice was just a tiny scratch on the surrounding silence.

"Please . . . ?"

"I do something bad to you sometime, kid?" the half-breed asked. "Or was it I just scared the shit out of you?"

He was about twenty. Youthfully good-looking, with clear skin and blond hair. In a vague sort of way, he resembled Jamie. Except that Jamie had never been so afraid. Not that the half-breed had ever seen Jamie afraid. Maybe when the troopers had started to . . .

"I ain't never seen you before, mister!" the youngster said quickly, to interrupt Edge's futile line of thought that led so far back into the distant past. "And it was me scared myself when I thought I'd shot you for sure. You gotta believe me. You must've heard me countin'. See! Look, the can I put in the tree. I was practicin' my shootin'. I ain't much good and I wanna be. Good, that is. Look, can you see it?"

One of his raised arms moved and a finger was extended from a fist to point. Edge looked in the direction indicated and saw the can lodged in a tangle of mesquite branches. High and to the left of where he had been standing when the boy fired.

"Looks like you're in real need of some practice, kid," the half-breed growled. He eased the hammer to the rest and slid the Remington into its holster.

"Yeah, I know it!" the boy said fast. "I have to be the world's worst shot, but I'm real eager to learn. Every chance I get, I set up targets and try to hit them. But I know it's gonna take time. But I'm so damn anxious to be good, I just don't . . ." He lowered his arms, sat up and shook his head, his face showing a mournful expression. "Gee, I'm so sorry, mister. I didn't see you until it was too late. My folks always said I was like a bull in a china shop when I wanted to do somethin' real bad."

8

"And you sure shoot real bad," Edge muttered, moving to stand on the spot where he had been when the bullet exploded from the boy's gun.

"Never can curb my enthusiasm is how Pa used to put it," the boy moaned, continuing to shake his head.

"Yeah," the half-breed drawled, as he checked that the bullet scar in the juniper bark was on a line and level with his chest. "That can be the way of things. For a moment there, I almost died hole-heartedly."

Chapter Two

"NAME'S CLAYTON, Mr . . . ?"

"Edge," the half-breed supplied as he climbed with a grimace out of the dry wash and the boy got to his feet.

"Mr. Edge. Willard Clayton. Name on the wagon, that's just to impress the payin' customers. Least I can do after what happened is to offer you a cup of coffee. Or pull a tooth free, if any's botherin' you?"

He grinned and his features were even more reminiscent of Jamie.

"Coffee and my rump on something that ain't moving for awhile will be fine, kid," Edge replied. "I've been riding so long, when I'm in the saddle it feels like I'm sitting on a toothache."

"You got a horse, Mr. Edge? I didn't hear no animal close by. If I'd heard you ridin' up I wouldn't have—"

"Other side of the trees, kid. You weren't supposed to hear me. Makes it part my fault you almost killed me. But you ever point a gun at me again, make the shot count. Or you're dead."

Clayton swallowed hard as he got quickly to his feet, leaving the discarded handgun on the ground. "I'll get him for you. You got stuff with you? I've only got eatin' utensils, a mug and things like that for myself."

"Obliged."

The boy moved hurriedly and nervously away from the fire, still shocked by the near miss and not looking at the half-breed after a single anxious glance at the lean face lit by the light of the flickering flames.

After he had dropped down into the dry wash and gone through the timber, Edge squatted on his haunches at the side of the fire, checked that the boy's mug was clean and poured coffee into it. He sipped at the hot, strong drink without revealing any facial response to what he thought of it. His narrowed eyes looked at the gun and then the wagon and horses.

The final light of day had now followed the set sun down below the western curve of the mesa but the flames illuminated the campsite well enough. And he saw that the revolver was a British-made Tranter .45 six-shot with customized wooden grips. While the enclosed wagon was like many the half-breed had seen during his disenchanting stay in New York City, except for the carefully lettered wording painted in vivid gloss-red on the matt-black side— THE GREAT MARVO, MAGICIAN AND DENTIST. Like the gun and the wagon, the two-horse team looked well cared for.

"I guess the sign means you're better at magic than shooting?" Edge posed as he heard hooves set rocks rolling and turned to watch the youngster lead the mare up out of the dry wash.

Clayton's mind was obviously still anxiously preoccupied with recent events and he had to think for a few moments before he understood what Edge was talking about. "Oh, the *great* thing," he said as he moved the mare wide of the fire and hitched the reins to a rear wheel of the wagon. "If you're in the entertainment business, you have to have a name like that. Folks expect it. All right if I use your mug, Mr. Edge? Seein' as how you're usin'—"

"Looks like you keep your things clean, kid. Yourself included. So I don't figure I'll catch anything off you."

"And pick up my gun?"

"Long as you remember what I said about not pointing it at me again, no sweat."

"Thanks."

"No debt, either."

Edge watched the boy until Clayton had come to sit down across the fire from him and poured himself a cup of his own coffee. And now could see nothing of Jamie in him. Willard Clayton was a lot skinnier than the half-breed's brother had been. And his build lacked the muscular development, his skin did not have the deep tanning which had marked out Jamie as a prairie farmer who worked long hours in the open air under the unpredictable Iowa skies. This boy's hair was definitely blond, whereas Jamie's coloration was sandy. The eyes of the youngster across the fire were brown and . . . Edge vented a low grunt of vexation as he realized he could not recall the color of his dead brother's eyes.

"You say somethin', Mr. Edge?" Clayton asked.

"Nothing."

"Oh."

Under the frock coat, the boy was dressed in a brown and white check shirt and well-cut pants that looked as if they were part of a tailored suit. There was a black string tie neatly knotted at the collar. Both his gunbelt and the holster held at the belly were old and there was a bullet in every loop. His boots were high of heel and he did not wear spurs. On his way to get the half-breed's mare he had dusted off his clothing.

"See, I want to be a gunfighter. What I do now, that don't appeal to me at all. It was just that when my Pa died, it seems right I should take over what he did. He spent years gettin' me ready to do that."

"Following in his footsteps to the Promised Land is what appeals to you, Willard?" the half-breed asked.

The boy grimaced and, just for part of a second as the expression was forming on his features, it could

13

have been a ghostly replica of Jamie's face which Edge saw through the distorting effect of shimmering heat rising from the fire. "Way I've been told, the best live the longest. And they live highest off the hog. Stands to reason, it seems to me."

"Stands to reason old men lie about their lives, Willard. Specially to over-eager kids."

"Everyone's entitled to their own opinions, Mr. Edge," Clayton said, piqued. "And to live their own lives."

The half-breed nodded. "For as long as they want to, God willing."

Clayton seemed satisfied to have reached this degree of agreement and he finished his coffee at a swallow. "You want some more?" he offered. "Because I have to get movin' now. I plan to do a show in Freedom at eight o'clock tonight."

Edge topped up his mug, emptied the rest of the coffee onto the ground and held out the pot toward the boy as Clayton got to his feet. "Freedom?"

The youngster showed surprise. "Town about five miles southeast of here. Only town within two days ride of here. Ain't that where you're headed?"

"No."

"Well, if you do happen through there in the next couple of days, we can exchange mugs then. If you don't, it ain't important. Been nice meetin' you, Mr. Edge."

"I'll remember you for awhile," the half-breed answered, using his free hand to massage a bruised thigh.

Confident of fresh supplies close at hand, Clayton used water from a container in the rear of his wagon to wash out the coffee pot and mug. Then he unhitched the mare, led the animal across the hollow and retethered her to a clump of mesquite. He collected the can from where it was lodged in the timber and took it with him up onto the wagon seat. A single bullet had at one time penetrated two opposite curves of the target.

14

"If you change your mind about comin' to Freedom," he called across the hollow, "come see my show, Mr. Edge. Like I said, I don't enjoy my work, but I'm damn good at it."

"Obliged for the coffee."

"My pleasure."

"The simple kind's always the best."

Clayton made a clucking noise and flicked the reins to set the two-horse team into motion, up out of the hollow the way they were facing and then into a right turn, the boy driving by the light of the now risen three-quarter moon.

As he listened to the sounds of the wagon's progress go out of earshot, Edge rolled a cigarette and lit it; all the time listening for other noises in the night. Soon, there was only silence beyond the hollow with, down in the depression under the mesa, just the crackle of burning wood.

When he had first dropped onto his haunches at the fire, the half-breed had intended to use the flames to cook himself a meal. But the prospect of a change of diet in a restaurant of a nearby town persuaded him to suppress his hunger and he lit and smoked the cigarette. Alone and unmoving in the almost total silence, he relied entirely on his sense of hearing to warn him of approaching danger while his slitted eyes, glinting in the firelight, stared at a fixed point in the middle distance, not into the fire in the event that a threat might appear in the darkness, when a man could lose valuable time while his pupils adjusted to the night.

Jamie had been younger than Willard Clayton when he died; he had not yet celebrated his nineteenth birthday. He died badly, on a bright day in June 1865, a few hours before his elder brother—then named Josiah C. Hedges—rode home to the Iowa farmstead from the war. Six troopers who served under Captain Hedges in the Union cavalry had reached the farm ahead of their former commanding officer. There to put the crippled youngster

15

to agonizing death and burn the farm buildings, without learning the whereabouts of the money they knew the older brother had sent to the boy.

The troopers had left one of their own dead beside the corpse of Jamie Hedges in the yard of the burnt-out farm, providing a pointer, if one had been needed, to the killers the half-breed set out to track down. And track them down he did. And took his revenge against them. Using every skill which he—a one-time Iowa farm boy himself—had learned during the long, bitter and bloody years of the war between the States.

But when he brought his brutal vengeance hunt to a vicious end, he found himself as empty of triumph as when he learned that the Union defeated the Confederacy. And on this occasion, down on the Arizona-Mexico border strip, he lacked even the solace of a future pleasant in prospect. For in the act of trailing and finding the five former troopers who murdered Jamie, Josiah C. Hedges killed a man in Kansas who the authorities of that state felt did not deserve to die. Thus did the recently mustered-out Captain Hedges of the U.S. Cavalry become an outlaw named Edge—this name adopted after a mispronunciation by an enraged Mexican.

Wanted for murder and without a home to go back to or kin to offer him shelter, Edge accepted his lot as a drifting loner, asking favors of nobody and eking a living by selling his war-taught skills to whoever needed and could afford them.

On occasions he had attempted to put down roots and every now and then somebody had discovered that, deep inside his hard and implacable façade, there were remnants of a few of the finer human feelings. But always his attachments to a place or a person had been violently severed. Most brutally when his beautiful young wife had died, in circumstances that cruelly apportioned to him a large amount of the blame, which had embittered and hardened him still further, draining him of virtually the last vestiges of humanity and sinking these even deeper beneath his bleak and impassive surface.

He had taken up again his aimless drifting across the American West and the Mexican North, handling uninvited trouble as efficiently and coldly as he dealt with the violent men and events he was paid to combat. Gradually over the years—most of them bloodier and in many ways harder to endure than those of the war—the tenets of his code of life had been pared away. Until now, this man who sat beside a fire in the moon shadow of the curved mesa adhered inevitably to only two rules. If unwanted favors came his way, he always returned them. And he never hired his gun for the specific purpose of killing a man.

The fire died low and the chill of night dropped down into the hollow. With no new brushwood to devour, the flames did not crackle. So that the silence was total until Edge stood up and crossed to where the mare was hitched. As he rolled his shirt sleeves down over his hirsute arms, fastened them at the cuff and put on a knee-length black coat he had taken from his bedroll, the half-breed smiled, enjoying the utter stillness and total lack of human company, recalling how during his visit to New York City he had come close to relishing such a simple pleasure only amid the stands of timber and expanses of grass in Central Park.

Then he shook his head as he unhitched the mare and swung astride the saddle. New York was some two thousand miles away and a single event which happened in the city was all that should stick in his mind; for it was there that he had been granted an amnesty on the old murder charge. Which meant that he was no longer a wanted man who needed to be constantly moving, hiding his true identity under an assumed name.

He heeled the mare forward, up from the hollow between the tracks left in the dust by the wheels of Clayton's wagon. And he saw that the youngster was following an old and little-used trail which stretched straight as an arrow from east to west before it veered to the left at the curved mesa and then ran in a direct line again toward a huddle of hills three miles to the southwest. Edge rode in the same direction as the wagon had taken, trying to blot from his mind thoughts of what had happened two thousand miles away and several weeks ago. For it had never been his way to reflect deliberately upon the impossible. And it was certainly not possible for him to revert back from what he had become to anything approaching what he once had been.

His long ride from the East into the West had proved that. For when violence invaded the train by which he left the city, his responses had been those of Edge, not Josiah C. Hedges. Equally instinctive was the way he took a hand in the troubles of the Rosses in the Middle-West. Afterward he could have reached his old home in just a few days of riding. Or, in a matter of a few more days, returned to the farm where he and Beth had set up house. But he had not even briefly considered either alternative. Instead, he had pushed west and then south, waiting and watching for new opportunities to draw and use his Remington, Winchester or straight razor. Preferring the risk—as he doubtless always had done from those opening days of the war—that he could finish up a blood-spilt corpse rather than face up to the prospect of growing peacefully old with only the changing of the seasons to add variety to life.

Which brought into question what might have happened had Jamie not died so young. Or Beth had survived. Which in turn brought him, as the lights of a town showed ahead between the folds of two hills, full circle back to the futile exercise of considering the impossible.

A few yards beyond where the lights first came into view among the hillcrests, a wooden marker stood at the side of the trail, one end tapered to a point. Weather had not yet completely obliterated the

18

marker's words, which had been painstakingly burned into the surface with a hot branding iron. In the moonlight, Edge read: THIS WAY TO FREEDOM, STRANGER.

The mare whinnied and scraped at the ground with a forehoof, impatient to be on the move again after the rider had halted her so that he could rake his eyes along the faded lettering on the marker.

"Easy," the half-breed soothed, running a hand gently down the neck of the horse. "Nothing worthwhile comes just by following a sign."

As if sensing a break in the routine of long days in every weather trekking across a seemingly endless wasteland and cold nights in bleak camps under the stars, the mare wanted to be given her head. But the man in the saddle held her on a tight rein, to maintain the same even pace over the final half mile as he had demanded throughout the day.

This final stretch of trail—as underused as that behind the half-breed, for there were no outlying homesteads on this side of Freedom—made a gentle curve on a constant upgrade, between flanking low hills, the sides of which changed gradually from dusty soil to scrubland and then to grassy meadows. At the points where the grass began, fences had been erected of five strands of barbed wire strung between posts. Flocks of sheep grazed on the turf, the animals close to the trail scampered away with nervous bleats as the horseman rode slowly by.

Then the ground leveled out and Edge rode between the two farmhouses and their barns and shacks which flanked the start of Freedom's main street. It was a broad street, without sidewalks at this end, lined beyond the farms by small houses with gardens enclosed by picket fences. Lamp and candlelight gleamed from windows and smoke laden with the smells of cooking curled up from chimneys. There were shade trees in all the gardens and some of the householders grew flowers or vegetables while others neglected the rich-looking soil of their plots.

19

This section of the street ran for about a hundred and fifty yards into the commercial center of town, where the sidewalks began and the buildings—a mixture of old and new—were of stone as well as frame construction, a number of them rising to two storeys.

On the left a bank, a gunsmith, a dry goods store, a saloon called The Sheepman and the sheriff's office. Across from these a livery stable, the fire station, a drugstore, a stageline and telegraph office with just one wire strung between poles going south and a combination bakery and restaurant. Beyond this, the street forked, one spur running due south and the other curving away southeast. For short distances before these less broad streets became open trails running between barbed-wire-fenced grazing meadows for sheep, they were lined by more houses similar to those on the north side of town. While in the angle of the Y formed by the dividing of the main thoroughfare was the newest and largest building of Freedom. Two storeys high and constructed of stone, it had a lamplit, garishly painted sign on the roof which named itself as THE FOUR ACES HOTEL, Prop. Abraham Billings.

Light spilled brightly from every window at the front and along the splayed sides of the hotel. Also from over and under the batwing entrance doors, together with tobacco smoke and raucous sounds of piano music and talk and laughter. Parked in front of the hotel, to one side of the shallow steps which led up to the canopied entrance was the wagon of Willard Clayton, the two horses no longer in the traces.

During his slow ride into town, Edge was alone on the main street. He could hear the rowdier element of Freedom raising a little hell in the barroom of the hotel and glimpsed an occasional couple or a family group through the uncurtained windows of houses. As he angled the mare from the center of the street toward the livery on the right, he saw that the Sheepman Saloon and the freedom Restaurant and Bakery were also open for business, their windows misted by

20

condensation. And that a lamp glowed dimly in the law office.

As he swung down from the saddle, a latch scraped and one of the two big doors of the livery stable opened to spill a wedge of light and the shadow of a man out across the street.

"Evenin' to you, mister. Thought I heard the sound of business comin'."

He was about sixty, with silver hair, a dark and drooping moustache. There were no bottom teeth in his friendly smile. A couple of inches under six feet in height, he was well built, with bulging muscles contoured by the tight-fitting top part of his gray Long Johns with the buttons unfastened to show his hirsute chest, the hair as silver as that on his head.

"Heard right, feller," Edge replied as the man pushed the door open wider to allow the newcomer to lead his horse inside. "Feed and water and stabling for a night."

"And a set of new shoes, looks like to me. I'm town blacksmith. Only one for thirty miles in any direction."

"You set your charge because of that?" the half-breed asked, not aware of how cold the night had become until he was inside the livery and blacksmith shop and felt the heat from the cheerfully glowing forge.

There were a dozen stalls around two walls, half of them occupied. The smells in the place were of burning, coffee and horse droppings.

"Charge the same as Lloyd Day down at the Dry Springs stage stop who's my closest competition," the man answered, taking the reins and dropping down onto his haunches to check on the mare's shoes. He stood up and his smile was marred by a brief grimace as the move caused a pain in the small of his back. "And if you rode down there on this animal she'd be four-footed lame."

"You made a sale, feller."

"Do her in the mornin' if that's all right, mister.

21

By the time I get your horse bedded down, be time for the magic show."

"No sweat," the half-breed allowed, working on the ropes which held his bedroll in place behind the saddle.

"I'll take care of all that, mister. No extra charge. Unless you want to take anythin' along with you."

"Obliged. Just this." Edge slid the Winchester from his boot. "Good food in the restaurant down the street?"

"It'll keep a man's belly and backbone from touchin'. You'll get better fed by the Widow Emmons that runs a boardin' house on First next to the church—that's the street that goes off Main to the right of the Four Aces. Three square a day comes with a clean room and no bugs in the bed."

"That better than the hotel?"

The grin evaporated and the broad shoulders were shrugged as the man took the saddle and bedroll off the horse. "Fancier rooms there and no bugs in the beds that I've heard about. But any man rents a room gets the bite put on him. On account a female comes with the bed and bureau and chair." He spat into the forge fire as he led the horse over to a stall. "Real fine lookin' females. And Rosie Pride charges high for them. On account of she ain't got no competition for her service closer than fifty miles any way you ride outta Freedom." He shut the mare into the stall. "That kinda hunger and the kind a man has for gamblin' is all that's catered for at the Four Aces."

"Obliged for the advice."

"No trouble, unless you put it around I steered you clear of that place. Abi Billin's that owns it wouldn't be best pleased with me if he knew—"

"No sweat, feller," Edge cut in as he moved to the door, the Winchester canted to his left shoulder. "My stake wouldn't run to cathouse comforts anyway."

"Hey, don't you let that one eyed, nose-pickin' Abi Billin's hear you call his place that! He's got some mean muscle workin' for him and—"

"Obliged again."

"And one other thing, mister!" the liveryman called as Edge pushed open the unlatched door. "Sheriff Gould don't mind men totin' handguns in holsters but he won't take kindly to you walkin' around Freedom with that rifle."

The half-breed pursed his lips. "Be all right in this town to spit if I get a bad taste in my mouth, feller?"

This was greeted with a hollow laugh. "Sure ain't never heard of anyone gettin' beat up or arrested for doin' that, mister. No, sir. This here town of Freedom is well named, long as you stay outta law trouble and don't rub Abi Billin's up the wrong way. Just about anythin' goes."

"Good advice, stranger," a man on the street augmented as Edge stepped outside. A tall thin man dressed entirely in black, which made the brassy glint of the bullets in his gunbelt loops and the silvery glitter of the five-pointed star pinned to his vest seem more pronounced. "Comes from doin' the work he does, I reckon. The way Art Ely talks so much horse sense."

"Evenin', Huey," Ely greeted.

The lawman had a face to match his frame—long and lean. His bone structure was angular and he had deep-set eyes and sunken cheeks. He was somewhere between forty and fifty and all the lines engraved into his dark tinted skin had a downward tilt, suggesting that he seldom wore a smile to displace the morose frown he now showed.

"Goin' to be a good one, Art. What with the magic show and all. Providin' we don't have no trouble from unexpected quarters."

His dark eyes gazed fixedly out from their deep sockets into the impassive face of the half-breed.

"Arranged to have my horse taken care of, sheriff," Edge said evenly. "Now intend to eat, get cleaned up and sleep. Guess all that is like spitting in the street in this town?"

"Uh?"

"Ain't against the law."

There was movement on Freedom's streets now. As people emerged from the houses and headed for the Four Aces Hotel. Men, women and children, wrapped up in warm coats and scarves against the chill of the night air. Varying degrees of eager excitement showed on their faces. Several of the men called evening greetings to the sheriff, who ignored the friendly words to emphasize his scowl toward Edge.

"Just you bear in mind what I said about not wantin' any trouble from unexpected quarters, stranger," Gould rasped.

"Figure you do expect it from me, sheriff," Edge answered. "Only come, though, if anybody invites it. And not in quarters. Never do things by half measures."

"Won't, if you take Art's advice and keep the peace and stay out of Billin's way."

The lawman swung into a half turn and started along the street, now responding to the friendly words, tipping his Stetson to the women who smiled at him.

"Reckon that crack about quarters and half measures was lost on the sheriff, mister," Ely said as he stepped out of the livery behind Edge and closed the door, shrugging into a sheepskin coat he had taken from a hook on the wall. "He ain't the brightest lawman in these parts. Must've been someplace else when the good Lord was handin' out brains."

The half-breed pursed his lips as he moved along the street in the same direction as everyone else. Then he drawled, "Sounds like he might have been standing in line for a second helping of mouth."

Chapter Three

THE RECEPTION he had received from Sheriff Huey Gould was not a new experience for the half-breed. And he had learned to take in his stride such warnings from lawmen in small and peaceful towns. For he knew that to men with badges on their shirts and a conscientious regard for their sworn duty, he looked like trouble just waiting for a fuse to be lit. And in the case of the sheriff of Freedom, it sounded as if the man already had one such problem in the owner of the Four Aces Hotel.

"That's him, mister," Art Ely said in a rasping whisper. "Up there at the window of his room."

Most of the people in the street had made faster progress than Edge and the liveryman toward the front of the Four Aces. So that the two men were at the rear of a large gathering of local citizens when they came to a halt and Ely spoke.

The half-breed directed his narrow-eyed gaze over the heads of the excitedly noisy crowd toward the lighted window on the second floor, immediately above the hotel entrance. A man stood there, against the lamplight in the room but illuminated by that which lit the sign on the roof.

A man of about forty-five, six feet tall and of slim build. Dressed in a white suit, the jacket unbuttoned to show the gold watch-chain that was strung across the front of his blue vest. His shirt was a slightly paler shade of blue and he wore a cravat at his throat that was striped white and blue. He was hatless so that his slicked-down black hair, thinning at the

25

front, could be seen. His thin face was handsome in what might possibly have been a weak way had it not been for the black patch which shielded his right eye and gave him a somewhat mean look. The blackness of this patch and the band which held it in place was emphasized by the milky paleness of his blemish-free skin which was stretched taut over the prominent bone structure of his long face. From the distance over which Edge saw him, the man's eye looked dark in the depths of its socket.

For a few moments as Billings looked down upon the crowd gathered in front of his hotel, moving his head slowly from side to side to ensure that he missed nothing and nobody, he had the bearing of some European aristocrat reviewing a throng of people who were beneath him in more than the literal sense. Then he raised a heavily ringed left hand and prodded the index finger carefully into his right nostril.

"He's got more pull in this town than Huey Gould and he likes trouble even less," Ely amplified.

Billings twisted his finger back and forth, located something, extracted it, rolled it between finger and thumb and flicked it off to the side. Then immediately looked aristocratic again.

"Sure seems to keep his own nose clean," Edge answered as Billings's eye located him and scrutinized him for longer than anyone else in the crowd.

Ely glanced nervously around. "Hey, mister, it ain't done to comment on that habit he's got. Most of the time he don't realize he's doin' it and when somebody says he is——"

A burst of hand clapping and shouts of approval covered the liveryman's latest advice. This applause greeting the appearance of Willard Clayton at the thrust open batwing doors of the hotel. A brightly smiling, much heavier looking youngster than the one Edge had seen out by the curved mesa north of Freedom. Dressed in a newer frock coat at least three

26

sizes bigger than the one he traveled in and wearing a shiny top hat instead of the Montana peak.

The half-breed had to do a double-take before he realized that the boy's bulk had to be caused by the tools of his magician's trade concealed under the coat. And he also spotted, in a brief moment while Clayton was bowing in response to the fulsome welcome, a look of deep-seated fear in the brown eyes—too intense to be termed stage fright.

"Ladies and gentlemen . . . and children!" the boy shouted, raising his arms and lowering them to signal that the applause should end. And as the noise became subdued, his eyes, which no longer showed fear, swept across the face of Edge and he smiled more brightly in recognition. The two exchanged slight nods, then Clayton raised a hand to his jaw, opened his mouth, and an egg rolled out over his lower lip. Which produced a further burst of applause over which he had to shout. "Thank you, thank you! I'm real pleased to be here in this delightful little town of yours and I'm overwhelmed by your welcome! Marvo's my name and I sure hope you'll think I'm worth callin' great! What I aim to do here and now is demonstrate a few little illusions to entertain you! If they do, for the small price of two bits you can come into this fine establishment and witness some amazin' feats of the magician's art which I feel will truly astound you! So watch very carefully, kind people of Freedom!"

As he finished speaking he pressed both hands to his chest, threw them forward, snapped his fingers and two multi-colored lengths of silk fell from his previously empty fists.

Edge glanced up at the window above the hotel entrance porch under which Willard Clayton was performing. And saw that the one-eyed Billings had retreated from view. Then he saw the man again, standing with two others and three women at the batwings behind the young magician. The men were

27

dressed city-style like Billings. The women—all in their mid-twenties—had heavily painted faces and showed powdered shoulders and the top swellings of their breasts above the bodices of vividly colored gowns.

"What the hell's happenin' here, Art!" a man slurred.

He was one of three, dressed in work clothes, who had staggered across the street from the Sheepman Saloon. Stockily built with a leathery skin and a complexion mottled by heavy drinking. Like his two taller, less drunken-looking companions, he was about thirty.

"Just shut up and watch, Chris!" Ely growled at the man who tugged at his arm. He spared the man just a brief angry glance before returning his intent interest toward Clayton—who had removed his top hat and was pulling a vast array of small toys from it, tossing each one toward a joyful child in the audience. "Look and you'll find out."

"How the hell can I see over this lousy mob?" Chris snarled. "I ain't no long streak of pi—"

"Mind your language!" the liveryman cut in bitingly without taking his fascinated gaze away from the beaming Clayton at the front of the cheering crowd. "There's women and children present!"

"Except that the women that interest me are inside the Four Aces!" Chris came back in the same snarling tone as before. But louder, so that some of the people at the rear of the gathering heard his words and turned to scowl at the distraction. The man leered at the women among them. "You got nothin' to worry about, you old strait-laced—"

"Chris!" the man on his right interrupted suddenly sobered by the look he saw on Art Ely's face as the scowling people returned their attention to Clayton. These people were grateful they could join in the applause of the crowd as the young magician completed this part of his act; and thus withdraw from the center of a potential arena of trouble.

28

The other tall man who was on Chris's left also seemed abruptly untouched by the effects of hard liquor. "Yeah, Chris!" he urged as he laid a hand on the short drunk's shoulder. "Let's go have a few more snorts. Rose's girls'll be just as beautiful and willin' when all this is over—"

"Leave go of me, frig it!" Chris yelled, shaking violently free of the restraining grip and taking a backward step from between his two anxious companions. "I drink when I wanna drink and with a place like the Four Aces in town I screw when I wanna screw! And now I wanna screw!"

Once more a noisy reception for the performer as he drew a live rabbit from his hat kept the drunk's words from reaching the ears of all but the back row of the audience. And these people pressed forward, which caused a chain reaction throughout the crowd and triggered a series of mild protests and automatic apologies to be voiced.

"You're drunk, Wilkes!" Ely said forcefully. "And it ain't the first time you got that way and tried to spoil other folks' pleasure! Do what Lee and Travis want and go on back to the Sheepman! On account that if you don't, old as I am, I'll make it so women won't interest you for a long time!"

Willard Clayton had faltered in his act as the crowd rippled and made sounds which were not in response to an illusion. And then all noise except for the voice of the angry and distinctly speaking Art Ely trailed into silence. So that the words of his threat rang out loud and clear across the thickly peopled intersection of Freedom's three streets.

"Ladies and—" the young magician called in an attempt to regain his audience as they swung their nervous attention away from him.

"You mean like you, you shriveled-up oldster?" Chris Wilkes taunted with a scornful grin. "I hear tell that's why that well-stacked young wife you had run off to Denver! Because you ain't got what it takes to keep a woman—"

Just as Wilkes's contemptuously hurled words had curtailed Clayton's opening, so an animalistic snarl of rage from Ely brought the drunk to a premature full stop. But whereas the magician on the hotel stoop froze and gazed helplessly around, the liveryman followed his venting of high anger with a fury-powered lunge into movement.

Wilkes was standing a full six feet away from Ely, who had turned only his head toward the younger man as the taunt was voiced. But in what seemed like less than a second, Ely whirled and threw himself toward Wilkes. Away from where Edge continued to stand in an attitude of casual relaxation, the Winchester canted carelessly to his left shoulder. As Lee and Travis sidestepped with grunts of shock and what was now the front row of the audience pressed against the people behind them and gasps and shouts rose from the crowd.

The grin of scorn remained fixed upon the liquor-sodden face of Wilkes until one of Ely's tight-clenched fists struck between the arms he raised in defense and landed with a sharp crack of bone against bone on the point of his bristled jaw. Then, with a grimace of pain as he staggered backward, tripped over his own feet and was sent sprawling down to the dusty street, he was gripped by a rage which matched that of his attacker.

The momentum of Ely's powerful lunge almost caused him to go down on top of his victim. But, as he teetered, body bent far forward, he flailed his arms frantically and managed to pull himself upright.

"Atta boy, Art!" a man in the crowd yelled enthusiastically. "About time that loud-mouthed trouble-maker was taken down a peg or two!"

"Cut it out! Let me through! You men back there quit this! Let me through, damnit!" shouted Freedom's lawman who caused violent movement in the crowd of people as he forced a way through the press.

"I'm all done if he's done," Ely said breathlessly in

30

a whispering tone that only Edge, Lee, Travis and the closest people in the crowd could hear.

Wilkes, too, if he had been in a receptive mood. But his all-engulfing fury allowed no opening to outside influence except the sight of the tall, silver-haired liveryman whom he saw towering above him as he started to raise his back off the ground. And the silent snarl he displayed on his unshaven, purple-tinged face was mute testimony to this.

Like Ely, his companions and most of the other local residents of this town in the center of a sheep-raising area, Wilkes wore a fleece-lined-and-trimmed topcoat. But unlike the other men in general, Ely in particular, the man now seated on the street wore a gunbelt with a Frontier Colt in the holster.

"Done!" he shrieked at the now impassive liveryman. "I ain't even got started."

He twisted to the side and pressed a hand into the dust to lever himself onto his feet.

"Your choice," Ely rasped. And lashed out with a kick, the toe of his scuffed boot connecting beneath Wilkes's jaw.

The no-longer-drunk man half rose with a strength not his own. Then fell heavily again, too paralyzed by pain to break the force of the impact.

"Quit it, I told you!" Gould yelled as he burst out from the crowd and came to an abrupt halt.

Men—and some women—in the crowd who agreed with the first cry of approval for what Ely was doing were now shouting encouragement for the liveryman to follow through on his success.

"Get him!"

"Stomp the bastard into the ground!"

"Show him we don't want his kind on the streets of Freedom!"

"Please, ladies and gentlemen!" Willard Clayton tried again. "Look, I can—"

He unfolded an arm from the front of his coat and a bunch of artificial flowers appeared to sprout from his palm. Mere anxiety and confusion about what

31

was distracting his audience were replaced by moments of quivering fear. Just then Abi Billings emerged from the hotel and hooked a hand briefly over the youngster's shoulders.

"You want some of that, Wilkes?" Ely demanded in the same rasping tone. And he took a step closer as the younger man, blood spilling over his lower lip, fought himself up into a splayed-leg sitting posture again.

"You're through, you ball-less old sonofabitch!" Wilkes screamed, spraying blood droplets.

"Don't be crazy, Chris!" Lee roared, backing further away from the line between Ely and Wilkes. Forcefully enough to collide hard with Gould and send the lawman stumbling and cursing into the crowd.

"Emmylou ain't worth it!" Travis called, his voice husky with fear. And his sentiments drew Ely to snap his eyes away from Wilkes and glare with renewed anger at a new target.

Ely, Edge realized, must have seen the man with the blood-run jaw start to claw the Colt from the holster. But the insult directed at Emmylou—the old man's young wife—took precedence in his mind.

"That girl's better than all—" Ely started.

He spoke into another tense silence which began as all the watchers realized what had caused Lee and Travis to shout at Wilkes. And broke off as the revolver shot cracked.

Silence again for part of a second. Until the bullet thudded into the closed door of the Freedom Restaurant and Bakery. The lead could only have missed Ely's turning head by a fraction of an inch; exploded by a man unable to take careful aim as he shook his own head to try to ease the pain and perplexity caused by the second blow to his jaw.

Then the screams and the gasps and the shouts filled the chill night air. As the crowd pressed backward, carrying the cursing Sheriff Gould with it.

Wilkes cocked the hammer of his Colt and spread

a grin of evil triumph across his features. Supremely confident of a killing shot with his second bullet as, with an anguished cry of defeat, Art Ely chose to stumble backward instead of hurling himself at the man with the gun.

All sound except for the liveryman's frantic intake of breath was again abruptly, shockingly curtailed.

"He ain't armed! You'll hang!"

The first three words which Gould roared came before the gunshot. The second two, husky in tone, followed it.

Ely fell hard to the ground. Going to the side. With a cry of alarm rather than pain. And all but a single pair of eyes looked on in terror as a black hole appeared in the center of Chris Wilkes's forehead. The man measured his stocky frame on the street again, his once-fired gun sailing through the air— powered by an involuntary throwing action as he flung both arms to the side. As the back of his head impacted with the ground, a gout of blood exploded from the bullet wound and rained in light reflecting droplets back down onto his face.

Slowly, in the stretched seconds which followed the killing, all eyes raked away from the spread-eagled corpse to look at the tall, lean man with coldly glinting blue eyes who had fired the second shot. He stood in an evenly balanced half-crouch, half-turned from the waist toward his victim. Both arms extended. In the left was the uncocked Winchester which he had used to send Ely crashing to the street. In the right a Remington revolver, blue smoke wisping from the muzzle, hammer back in the event that another shot would be needed.

But Edge saw in the next instant that one shot had been enough to kill Wilkes. Then, after his heavily hooded eyes had raked the scene and he was sure there was no immediate danger from other sources, he eased the hammer forward, slid the Remington into its holster and straightened up.

"Gee, mister!" the liveryman croaked as he

started to get painfully to his feet. "He'd have killed me for sure."

"What I figured."

Travis and Lee had hurried over to crouch beside the sprawled form of their buddy.

"Chris is dead, sheriff!" Lee said with a noisy gulp.

Gould had struggled clear of the crowd again, his expression so morose now it looked almost moribund. "Somebody was bound to be," he said in a voice that matched the set of his thin features and his dark garb. "Way it turned out, no law was broke. Not like if Chris Wilkes had gunned down Art who wasn't armed."

The dark eyes of the lawman as they came to rest on the half-breed's impassive face showed a momentary deep-seated resentment.

"Couldn't agree with you more, Huey!" Billings called, the accent in his words placing his origins far to the east and south of this Nevada Territory-California border area.

There was a murmuring of other voices, all contributing to a general sound of further agreement.

"Though I can't for the life of me see," the lawman went on, "why this stranger felt the need to interfere. To my mind he don't look like no—"

"Did it for my horse," Edge drawled.

"Uh?" Ely and Gould said in unison as the liveryman was eased to the side by the white suited Billings emerging from the crowd.

"Needs shoeing. And this feller is the only blacksmith within thirty miles of here."

"That certainly is right, sir," Billings said enthusiastically. "Which means you did the whole town a favor."

This was greeted with a more fervent cheer than any Willard Clayton had received during his performance.

"Well, I guess I know now where that leaves me in the opinion of this town!" Ely muttered with bad

34

grace as he scanned the faces of his fellow citizens.

"Alive, sir!" Billings supplied with a bright grin as he slapped him on the back.

Ely made a deep throated sound of disgust and glanced from the smiling face of the hotel owner to the impassive set of the half-breed's features. "I ain't sayin' I ain't grateful, but—"

"Don't be, feller," Edge told him evenly. "Put it down to one of the things I do for Art."

Chapter Four

"YOU'LL TAKE a drink in my establishment, sir?"
Billings invited. "On the house. And perhaps you'd
care to stay at the Four Aces if you have business to
hold you in Freedom?"

He was ushering Edge ahead of him as the crowd
divided to allow them free passage to the steps leading up to the hotel stoop. Willard Clayton was still in
front of the batwings, looking lost and lonely and not
a little nervous.

"Hello again, Mr. Edge," the young magician
called down.

The half-breed nodded to him. "Take a drink and
pay for it, feller. Only figure to be in town the one
night. While my horse gets what's needed and I rest
up. Single-bed sleeping style."

He glanced at Billings and saw that the one-eyed
man was resentful of his attitude, but only allowed it
to show for a moment before the grin was back in
place, as firmly fixed as ever.

"Guess Art Ely steered you to the Widow Emmons's place? Martha Emmons is Emmylou's mother
and she and Ely feel real sorry for each other about
that girl running off the way she did."

Up close, only one of the three women at the
batwings was as attractive as she had looked from
the rear of the audience. She was an oval-faced
blond with eyes only a shade darker than her vivid
green dress. Her skin looked as if, under the paint, it
were soft and clear enough not to need the cosmetics.
Her teeth as she parted her full lips in a warm smile

37

were very white and perfectly matched. She had slender arms, a narrow waist and finely shaped breasts, at least in the contoured cups of the gown's bodice.

The two brunettes who flanked her were of the same age but had either been more ill-used or had taken less care of themselves than the blond. One had a sallow complexion and the other was blemished, her imperfections extending across her chest and down into the valley between her breasts. Both had brown eyes that looked glazed by world-weariness and as smiles spread over their faces there was a longing behind the expressions to be elsewhere doing something different.

"Welcome, Mr. Edge," the blond said. "I'm Rose Pride. And these are two of my young ladies. Liz and Joanna. Or there's eight more if you do not—"

"He just wants a drink, sweetheart," Billings told her.

"Whatever your pleasure is, sir," Rose said, her genuine-looking smile appearing to remain as warm as ever.

Meanwhile the two whores shrugged their indifference to the stranger's lack of interest in their wares and swung around with a rustle of petticoats to saunter back into the depths of the hotel's big bar room.

"Mr. Billings," Willard Clayton called nervously as the one-eyed man held open one of the batwings for Edge to enter. "I do a good act, sir. But I figure it's gonna be hard to follow the spectacle of a man gettin' shot down on the open street."

Both Edge and Billings turned to look beyond the artificially bulky frame of Clayton at the scene on the intersection before the hotel. The crowd had dispersed now, family groups hurrying away along all three streets, as if the parents considered that speed would aid in wiping from the memories of their children the scene of violence which had been witnessed. A number of men, alone or in pairs or threes, were ambling diagonally across the intersection toward the dingy façade of the Sheepman Saloon. Another group of men stood at the foot of the steps, obviously waiting for Billings to declare his place open again for normal business. Sheriff Gould and another man were leading Lee and Travis—these two with the body of Wilkes slung between them—along the First Street fork.

"Don't even try, son," the one-eyed man replied with a nod. Another smile. "But tomorrow's another day, uh? Come on in." And he beckoned to the men at the foot of the steps. "You, too. First drink on the house. For those that ain't averse to bein' treated, that is."

The warmly smiling Rose linked her arm through that of Edge and tugged him gently across the threshold of the Four Aces. "Bet you're a real wet blanket at Hallowe'en, Mr. Edge," she accused lightly.

"How's that, ma'am?" the half-breed asked, aware of her subtle perfume as he looked around the bar room across which he was allowing himself to be steered.

"It's miss. But I like plain Rose best. I mean you don't go for . . ." she laughed a gentle laugh, ". . . tricks or treats."

The big, high-ceilinged room was warm with the heat from two large pot-bellied stoves, one at either end. The long bar ran along the rear wall. There were a dozen-and-a-half tables with chairs around them. At one end of the bar was a small platform with a piano, some chairs and music stands on it. At the other end a broad staircase rose to the upper floor. The white-painted walls were hung with gilt framed paintings of reclining nudes wearing coy expressions. Suspended from the ceiling were two clusters of kerosene lamps. The floor was of scuffed boarding.

Two Negroes were behind the bar and another sat on a stool at the piano. The nine whores were scattered among the tables, some alone and without drinks and the rest with men who had apparently paid for whatever was in the glasses in front of them.

39

There were some twenty paying customers in the barroom—keeping company with whores, intent on playing cards or simply drinking.

Both the help and the customers eyed the half-breed with great interest as Rose Pride took him among the tables to the bar counter.

"Come on, folks, liven up this place!" the good-looking madam shouted.

"Yeah, do that!" Billings augmented as he reached the bar and made a fist of one ringed hand to bang it down on the top. "A free drink for everyone! Make some music, Sam!"

The black pianist started a grin and began to thump at his keyboard. Then the bartenders matched his expression as they turned to lift bottles and glasses from the shelves. While the established patrons of the place were more vocal in their responses as they rose noisily from their tables, bolting down their old drinks so that they had empty glasses for the free refills.

The warmly-clad group from Willard Clayton's disintegrated audience entered and moved across the barroom apprehensively, huddled together and casting nervous glances about them, obviously ill-at-ease strangers in a new environment.

But nobody looked quite so discomforted as the young magician who was the last to enter the Four Aces and trod a lonely path from the batwinged entrance to the stairway.

Edge caught sight of Clayton as he raised the shot glass to his lips and swallowed the rye at a gulp. Billings saw the boy, too and shouted above the clamor of piano music, loud talk and gusty laughter, "Hey, son! You're included! Come on over here and take a drink!"

Clayton tried to mask his anxiety with a wan grin and then his mouth moved to form words. But he realized his voice did not penetrate the noise and he over-emphasized a yawn and used a fisted hand to mime rubbing the grit of weariness from his eyes. His

40

other hand was clutched around the paraphernalia of his act, including the ears of the docile rabbit.

"Suit your friggin' self!" Billings rasped, low but forceful, his lips pulled into a thin line and his one uncovered eye glinting with anger. And this expression—as far removed as it was possible to get from the warm friendliness he had exhibited a moment ago—was directed toward Edge as the half-breed dropped a silver dollar on the bartop and asked the nearest Negro, "You can make change, feller?"

There was a mirror in back of the shelves of bottles and glasses behind the bar and Edge saw Billings's face in profile. He also saw the pretty features of Rose Pride visited briefly by anxiety, then show a good imitation of her previous good humor.

"Mr. Edge and the kid are both tired, Abi," she said hurriedly. "Nobody reaches this town without a long, hard ride. Tomorrow's another day, ain't that what they say?"

"And tomorrow the Sheepman will still get most of the business," the one-eyed man growled, but as he spoke managed to suppress his ill-feeling and raise an unconvincing smile. "Rose is right, Edge. Get some sleep. You're welcome to stay here. Or go to Martha Emmons's place if you're set on it. But come morning, I'd appreciate the opportunity of a word with you, sir?"

He nodded to the waiting bartender who dropped the silver dollar into a pocket of his leather apron and counted out change in nickels and dimes.

"Never drink hard liquor before noon, feller," Edge said as he pocketed the change. "Be at the restaurant for breakfast soon as it opens. Then at Ely's livery for as long as it takes to shoe my horse."

By now Billings had repaired all the damage which his sudden anger had caused to his demeanor. "Breakfast at the Freedom Restaurant at seven then? And after you hear what I have to say, maybe you won't be in too much of a hurry to get your horse shoed?"

Edge showed no response to the man. But he touched the brim of his hat toward the madam and said, "Miss Pride."

Then he turned from the bar and moved back among the tables toward the batwings. The noise level in the stove-heated, tobacco-smoke-and-perfume-smelling barroom had now been reduced to about the same as it had been before Willard Clayton began his performance out on the stoop. Two card games were restarted, the piano player was thumping out the least raucous of the only three tunes he appeared to know, the most hopeful of the whores were laughing at everything their potential customers said to them and money and liquor were being exchanged regularly across the polished bartop.

As he reached the batwings and began to push open one of them with his free right hand, Edge sensed hostile eyes looking at him and he glanced over his shoulder. And located the man who wished him ill-will just before the pair of brooding eyes were averted to peer too intently down at the surface of a glass of beer—long untouched and flat. The man was about thirty, prematurely bald, with a vee-shaped scar on the right side of his jaw. He was sharing the table, closest to the piano player, with the other expensively and stylishly dressed man whom Edge had first seen standing with Billings and Rose Pride during Willard Clayton's performance.

The half-breed raked his narrowed eyes across the rest of the room and its occupants and saw other isolated areas where tension lurked in the general atmosphere of conviviality.

Billings was talking fast to the now anxious-looking madam. The group of men who had come in off the street were still gathered together at one end of the bar, their talk and free drinks exhausted, wearing expressions which suggested they wished they had never entered. And, at the top of the stairway above the group, Willard Clayton stood in the fringe of light from one of the lamp clusters—peering down at the one-eyed man and Rose Pride with blatant hatred, until he realized he had been seen. Then fear—as strong as that which had shown after he almost shot Edge—flooded across his face. He searched frantically for whoever was watching him, spotted the half-breed at the hotel entrance, drew not an iota of comfort from this and whirled to hurry out of sight along the hallway.

"I told Art Ely to have your horse ready first thing in the mornin', stranger."

The morose-looking, mournful-toned, black-clad Sheriff Gould was coming up the broad steps to the stoop as Edge pushed out through the batwings. Beyond his tall, lean figure, the main street of Freedom was deserted, the glint of moonlight on dark windows seeming to emphasize the biting chill of the night. Light but no noise spilled from the Sheepman Saloon and down on the residential stretch of the street a few of the house windows showed lights.

"Obliged," Edge replied as the batwings flapped closed behind him and his eyes, bleaker and colder than the night, shifted their unblinking gaze from the darkened façade of the restaurant to the unfriendly face of the lawman.

"Favor for the folks of Freedom, not you," the sheriff growled. "Your kind ain't welcome here."

"What kind is that?"

"The kind that lives by the gun."

There was a shuffle of feet on boarding behind Edge and the doors of the Four Aces swung open ahead of the men who had reached a decision to leave after the free round of drinks.

"That ain't fair, Huey," a short, round-faced, bug-eyed man of about fifty muttered. "Hadn't been for the stranger, it would've been Art we'd be buryin' tomorrow instead of that no-good Chris Wilkes."

"That's right!" a man ten tears older and with a bulging belly that threatened the fastenings of his coat agreed. "And don't you pretend you ain't glad there won't be no more trouble from Wilkes, either."

43

Gould glowered at the two men who had spoken and the others who, from the looks on their faces were obviously in agreement with the opinions expressed. "I already stated clear and plain this stranger didn't commit no crime. Way it was with Art Ely unarmed and all. But there ain't been no gunplay on the streets of Freedom since I was elected sheriff. Until tonight. And if this stranger wasn't present, I reckon I could have taken care of the quarrel without no one gettin' shot."

"I ain't so sure—" somebody started to say.

"I am!" the lawman cut in grimly. "Chris Wilkes was trouble, but I could handle him. Could've tonight, without any help from this fast gun. You men go on home now."

Gould came purposefully up the steps, brushed past the half-breed and went in through the batwings as the group of men parted to allow him access.

"Huey means well for the town, mister," the man with bug eyes said. "And it's true what he says about keepin' gunplay off the streets of Freedom."

The youngest of the group, who was also the thinnest and tallest, cleared his throat with a nervous sound. "That don't mean Mr. Tuttle here thinks you're the kind that causes that brand of—"

"No sweat," Edge replied as the man with prominent eyes swallowed hard at the realization that his defense of Sheriff Gould might have been misconstrued. "Ely hadn't been the blacksmith, it wouldn't have been my business."

"What is your business?" a man with a deep voice asked as Edge started down the steps.

His companions made shushing noises at him. And when the half-breed halted and looked back up at the stoop, it was obvious that the others were looking at the middle-aged man with red sideburns and chin-whiskers and it was he who had posed the question.

"It's just that I'm the gunsmith here in Freedom," the man who was the center of anxious attention said. "And if you . . ."

44

His voice trailed away to silence under the steady, slit-eyed gaze of Edge.

"Guess you carry a stock of shells, feller?"

An eager nod. "Yes, sir. For that Winchester and your Remington revolver both."

"Then you are a—" the bug-eyed Tuttle began.

"Man who makes an honest dollar any way he can," Edge interrupted.

The one with the red whiskers cleared his throat again. "Whatever, sir, we're mighty grateful for what you done. Most folks in Freedom will feel the same, 'cept for Lee and Travis and Jonas Cochran over to the Sheepman. We're all glad to see the back of that troublemaker Chris Wilkes."

The half-breed shook his head and sighed. "Gratitude's the same as money, feller. Only accept it when I earn it. Was on my own account that tonight I did some troubleshooting."

Chapter Five

THE CLAUDE R. Emmons Boarding House was a two storey building of frame construction between the Freedom Elementary School and the Episcopalian Church. There was a wooden shingle nailed to the door, with the paint which formed the lettering peeled and faded. This door set between two windows, one of which showed light beyond the drape curtains, was reached by a cracked and crumbled cement walk which ran between neglected flower beds. A few uprooted paling which had once formed a fence between the property and the street were scattered across the hard-packed soil of the garden.

"Who is it?" a woman called, shrill and nervous, in response to the sound of the half-breed's knuckles against the door. "It's late."

"Four Aces's still open to rent rooms, ma'am," Edge drawled. "But Ely the blacksmith said your place is better. For a man that wants to eat and sleep."

"You the travelin' dentist man or the other stranger?" With each nervous word she spoke she came closer to the other side of the door.

Edge sighed as a slight but very cold breeze sped down the main street from the north and shifted the long hair at his shoulders. "It matter, ma'am?" he wanted to know.

"If you're the tooth-puller, I hear tell he's got rabbits. I don't take in no animals!"

47

"Only thing I pull out of my hat is my head, Mrs. Emmons."

"Then you're the other one." There were sounds of bolts being pulled and a chain being rattled. "The man that put paid to Wilkes after he said bad things about my Emmylou."

The door was folded inward and she held a lamp to see her caller, but the cone of light also fell upon herself. She was closer to fifty than to forty. Short and heavily built, her thick, almost figureless frame wrapped in a crisp gray coverall. She had a round, pale face with dart button eyes, a snub nose and a pouting mouth. Her hair was held in a severe drawn-back style, mostly gray so that only a few streaks of its former blackness could be seen. She smelled fresh and clean. Like the interior of the house in back of her, in sharp contrast to its exterior.

She was still wary of her night-caller until he touched the brim of his hat. Then she set her lips into a firm line and nodded.

"Art told me about you. About what happened. You can stay. Two dollars for a day and a night. That includes three meals. No money back if you don't take any of them. Take a bath in front of the range in the kitchen if you're in need. And you look in need. There's heavy curtains at the window and a lock on the inside of the door. You want to eat tonight, there's only cold from supper. When I got a man boardin' here, women is the same as animals. I don't allow none in. Terms and conditions suit, mister?"

Edge smiled with his mouth. "In spades, ma'am."

She smiled in response, and the expression transformed her face from that of a soured woman who looked her age to one of good-humored youthfulness. "Good, young man. Then come in and treat this house as your home."

With a guest under her roof—she soon made it known that they were alone together in the big house—Martha Emmons launched into a cheerful

48

bout of chattering that should have left her breathless but did not. First while she showed him the spartanly furnished but spotlessly clean upper-front bedroom. Then as she served and watched him eat a meal of cold meat and salad. Next standing outside the kitchen door while the half-breed took a bath in the hip tub filled with water which had been heated in a half dozen pans while he ate supper. Finally during the time it took him to share coffee with her in the parlor of the house.

So that it was three hours after he crossed the threshold of the boarding house, and close to midnight, when he was able to strip down to his underwear and climb under the more than adequate blankets on the single bed.

Over-anxious to take advantage of having a quiet if not always apparently attentive listener, Martha Emmons tended to change the subject frequently, as if dragging from the back of her mind a series of topics which might recapture the half-breed's interest whenever it seemed to wane. But always she returned to pick up the threads of half-finished stories. Not always telling everything in chronological order but never missing out any detail of consequence.

Edge listened to her in conscious appreciation of the comfort he was enjoying, which he considered was worth more than the two dollars rent he was paying. Her food was good, the inside of her dilapidated house was warm and clean, there was a soft bed awaiting him upstairs and Martha Emmons accepted him for what he was. After the money had changed hands, she asked for nothing and—on the surface anyway—expected nothing.

But later, as he lay sprawled out under the blankets, the Winchester resting by habit against the wall close at hand, he began to have his doubts about the motives of the gregarious and motherly Widow Emmons. For almost all her talk had been about the town of Freedom which, he had judged for himself before he entered the boarding house, had more sources of potential trouble than the late and apparently unlamented Chris Wilkes. And, in retrospect, the sum total of what the woman told him had confirmed this.

Freedom had started out as a last-resort settlement community for sheepmen who had been driven off prime grazing land by cattle barons. A small, poverty-stricken town for the first few years. Just the houses on First Street, a single store and a frame church. But the families who founded Freedom knew the sheep business and by fencing of the pasture, careful use of available grazing and irrigation with water supplied from two deep wells the people prospered and the town grew.

The Emmons family were among the first to settle here, with Martha doing most of the work involved in raising sheep. Then, when the stage-line came through and Martha saw the need for catering to travelers, she also did her own and her liquor-addicted husband's share of the chores in running the boarding house. Ten years ago Buddy Emmons had taken every cent he could find in the house and left town on an early-morning stage. On the same stage was Jean Gould, wife of the town sheriff and, according to the way Martha told it, she and the lawman were the only people in town who did not consider it a coincidence. Gould rode out of town at noon that day and a week later news was received that the runaway pair were found tortured and mutilated—horrifically murdered—in the foothills of the Funeral Mountains. All Gould had said when he returned a few days later was that he had heard the same story. An Apache attack, everybody said.

Freedom continued to thrive and to expand. The stone church was built and Art Ely and Emmylou Emmons were the first to be married there, with the wedding feast held in the decorated but dingy surroundings of the Sheepman Saloon; the men who played the dancing music having to compete with the din of men working around the clock to build the Four Aces Hotel.

"Folks around here said they was an ill-matched pair, mister," Martha Emmons had murmured miserably. "And the way it turned out, there ain't no denyin' that. But at the time of the weddin', I figured Art was just the man for my Emmylou. A good deal older, a steady man and a hard workin' one. Just the kind to keep Emmylou in check. Way she was so wild, she was gettin' a bad reputation. But she up and left him a month after they was wed. Lit out on a stage, just like her father did. Which figured, her bein' so much like him."

The Four Aces Hotel had opened its doors for business by then and the single men of Freedom—and not a few of the married ones, too—had no need to try their luck with local fun-loving girls. Because, for a price, they were guaranteed to score at the hotel. Those with nothing to fear were able to enjoy the other pleasures and luxuries offered by Billings and those who needed to be discreet were allowed to enter and leave via a rear door.

For a while, Billings and Rose Pride did a roaring trade—at the expense of the other merchants and businesses in town. For prosperous but previously austere-living local farmers and trail-weary stage-line travelers chose to indulge themselves amid the luxury of the Four Aces, rather than accept the more modest facilities offered by the Sheepman Saloon and the Emmons Boarding House. Even the town's stores and the Freedom Bank suffered a decline in business as money for essential provisions was cut to the bone and hard-saved cash was withdrawn from many accounts.

But the boom for the Four Aces was not long lived. The novelty of its newness wore off and the sheen of its attractions grew dull. And, over the past three months, the hotel had become just one other business providing non-essential needs to the town and to the bulk of visitors and passing-through trav-

51

elers, for most of the stage line passengers were regulars who came and went on business.

Thus it was obvious, to all who understood the basic economics of running any enterprise as expensive to set up and operate as the Four Aces, that Abi Billings was not even paying his costs, let alone getting a decent return on his investment.

And Billings was not a man who took philosophically the loss of anything—especially money. It was particularly galling for him in this instance, since he knew there was a profit to be made. For he had made it, handsomely, during his initial period in business. Before the longer established competition won back its errant customers. The drinkers to the Sheepman, boarders to the Widow Emmons and women chasers to their wives and sweethearts.

In fair competition, the Four Aces retained a portion of the available trade. But not a large enough portion. And it was suspected by many in Freedom that a recent fire which destroyed a back room of the Sheepman had been set by one of Billings's henchmen. Certainly he had tried to buy out Martha Emmons. It was also a fact that he had vigorously lobbied prior to a recent town council meeting—offering cash and the free favors of the Four Aces girls as bribes—for votes on a proposition to advertise in big city newspapers for new settlers to come to Freedom. The vote had been narrowly lost.

That had been a week ago today and, in a drunken rage the night of the meeting, Billings had threatened dire consequences for all who stood in his way to making a success of the Four Aces. Since then he had hardly been seen, except for occasional glimpses of him at his room window, gazing viciously down at the main street of Freedom. Until tonight when his engagement of the young Willard Clayton had shown promise of attracting big business into the batwing doors of the Four Aces.

Why had the Widow Emmons told him so much? The potted history of the town and her personal opinions in regard to the characters of many of its citizens all seemed designed—in common with her direct references to the owner of the Four Aces—to make Abi Billings sound like the rotten apple in an otherwise choice barrel of fruit.

To give another viewpoint to the one she suspected he had heard from Billings (unaware that the half-breed and the hotel owner had not yet exchanged more than a dozen sentences)? This was likely—but to what end?

He slept, having used his recollections of what the woman said and attempting to guess at a reason for her talk as a means to attain sleep. Which was something he could usually do merely by closing his eyes. But then he did not usually take his rest under clean linen and blankets beneath a warm roof. The last time that had happened was in a New York City hotel.

The sound of a fist on the front door panel roused him.

"Who is it?" Martha Emmons called in a loud whisper.

"Art."

"All right, but keep your voice down. He may not be asleep."

Edge sighed and listened to the sounds of the bolt and chain being slid and lifted so that the door could be opened. Then:

"Come in. Quickly."

The door was closed and the fastenings were fixed. Footfalls in the hallway. The two of them went into the parlor and their voices became a constant murmuring sound. The half-breed had no need to check that the Winchester rifle was still in place against the wall beside the head of the bed. And he sank again into a shallow but restful sleep, confident that he would trigger awake in full command of all his senses should danger threaten.

But it was simply the gray light of pre-sunrise dawn pressing through the lace curtains at the room window which caused his eyelids to spring open. For no longer than five seconds he listened to the total silence which pervaded the town, then disturbed it himself by getting out of bed and dressing. Fully dressed for going out into the chill morning air, from the window he looked down on the deserted length of First Street, lined with a random selection of houses and stores on the opposite side. They were all time-stained and weather-ravaged, suggesting that First predated Main in the development of Freedom. Behind and above the buildings, sheep were stirring on a grassy hill slope which was sub-divided by barbed wire.

As he turned from the window he thought briefly of the events and talk of the previous night, but did not try to guess at why Billings should have intruded a big-city style house of pleasure on to such a peaceful and pastoral scene.

The landing was long and narrow with doors at regular intervals along both walls and the head of the stairway close to the rear end. As he moved unhurriedly toward the stairs, he heard the snores of a man and the deep breathing of a woman. Both from behind one door.

"Hear tell the older ones are so grateful, Art," Edge murmured with a wry smile as he started to descend the stairway.

He checked the case clock on the mantel in the parlor and saw the time was not yet six. Warmth from the range crept out under the kitchen door and he considered making some coffee and shaving off a night's growth of bristles while he drank it. But, despite all he had become, lacking so many of the normal human virtues, he was always reluctant to do anything that might be termed an abuse of hospitality.

So he used the privy out back of the house—having to slide two bolts and unfasten two chains to open the rear door—and then stepped through the gateway in a high fence which gave onto the unwalled churchyard humped by grassy mounds, each of these guarded by a wooden or stone marker.

As he went between the boarding-house fence and the side of the steepled church, he heard a wagon moving on the street. It was a buckboard drawn by a single horse, with Travis driving and Lee sitting beside him. As the rig was halted at the start of the walk which led to the arched entrance of the church, the two men looked down at the half-breed with nervous and hungover eyes. Like Edge, they were unshaven and it looked like they had slept in their clothes.

"We have to dig Chris's grave," the thinner, paler, more anxious Lee muttered.

Travis vented a growl as he swung down from the buckboard, reached into the back and took out two long-handled spades. "We don't have to tell him what we're about!" he rasped.

Edge spat out the final taste of a night's sleep and yesterday's cigarettes. The globule of saliva made an ugly stain on the hard-packed dirt of the street beyond the limit of the churchyard grass. "You fellers and your plans are about as interesting to me as that," he said evenly and swung away from the wagon to amble in the direction of the midtown area, the Winchester canted easily to his left shoulder.

One of the men started to rasp a soft but venomous retort. But then, like Edge, both of them looked up at the boarding house as the window of the half-breed's room slid noisily open. The Widow Emmons, a nightcap awry on her head and a blanket draping her shoulders and clutched at her throat called, "Mr. Edge! Ain't you gonna stay for some breakfast? Or coffee, at least?"

"No, ma'am," the half-breed answered, and glimpsed the mixture of anxiety and disappointment which spread across her face before he continued his unhurried progress along the street.

"Me and Trav wouldn't say no to some coffee, Mrs. Emmons!" Lee called.

"You two can go to the same place your friend Wilkes is already at!" the woman snarled, and banged the window closed to emphasize her anger.

The sun shafted a first ray of warm and bright light over the crest of the hill to the east of town as Edge reached the front of the Freedom Restaurant and sat down on the sidewalk. He rested the rifle across his thighs and rolled and lit a cigarette. All around him, the townspeople stirred from their beds to start living the new day. Smoke began to wisp from chimneys, windows and doors were opened, pots and pans and cutlery were rattled, babies cried, children shouted, dogs barked and chickens clucked. So that the regular thud of two spades digging into consecrated ground was soon lost amid the general hubbub of more usual morning sounds.

Men appeared on the streets and began to head out of town toward the surrounding pastureland, a few on horseback but most of them walking. Stores opened their doors for business, the owners or their helpers sweeping dust off the sidewalks out front of the premises. Friendly greetings were exchanged, with Edge pointedly excluded for most of the time. And while the bug-eyed man named Tuttle who ran the drug store and the chin-whiskered gunsmith spared curt nods for the half-breed when they saw him seated on the sidewalk, only a fleshy faced, broad-shouldered, totally bald man who banged open the doors of the Sheepman Saloon felt strongly enough to direct an embittered glower across the width of the street.

"It was Jonas Cochran's best customer you killed, mister," Art Ely said as he halted in front of Edge.

"Wilkes hadn't been such a hard drinking customer, he wouldn't be dead, feller."

"I hear Martha bent your ear some last night. That the reason why you plan to eat restaurant grub instead of her fine food?" He gave an involuntary belch and, in the not-yet-overheated air of early morning, Edge smelled ham and eggs on his breath.

"Ain't you got work to do?" the half-breed asked flatly, gazing coldly up at the silver-haired, black-moustached man.

"Good morning to you, sir!" Billings called out cheerfully in his Southern-accented voice as he came down the steps of the Four Aces. "And to you, Mr. Ely. Are we going to be three for breakfast?"

The blacksmith's expression changed from a strange brand of sad irritation to angry contempt as he looked back at Edge after a glance toward the broadly smiling hotel owner.

"So that's the way the wind blows!" he hissed between his top teeth pressed against his lower gums. Then he swung away from the rising half-breed and stalked angrily down the street toward his premises.

"Something upsetting our friend?" the one-eyed Billings asked.

"Seems he got the wind up over breakfast," Edge answered as a thin, middle-aged, nervously smiling Mexican latched open the restaurant door.

"*Buenos Dias*, Señor Billings. And Señor Edge. It will be a great pleasure to serve you. Enter, please."

The small restaurant was filled with sunlight which flooded in through the open doorway and penetrated with difficulty the dirt-smeared windows to either side. The half dozen tables were covered with food-stained cotton cloths, there was sawdust on the floor and the walls were spattered with countless blotches that were the remains of squashed insects. The air was heavy with the smells of baking bread, brewing coffee and simmering chili.

"Coffee and hot rolls, Ramon," Billings said as he indicated that Edge should sit at the table closest to the door. "And for you, sir?"

"Sounds fine," the half-breed answered, choosing the chair from which he could look out on the street.

"*Si*, right away, *señors*."

The Mexican left the room through a bead-curtained arch at the rear and Billings sat down to Edge's right. The moment he was seated, the gleam

57

of good humor left his uncovered eye and the set of his mouth altered from a smile to a sneer.

"The privy over at the Four Aces is cleaner than this place, Edge."

"I've already been this morning, feller."

Ramon reappeared, carrying a tray laden with the breakfast order. "Eat hearty, *señors*," he urged with enthusiasm when he had unloaded the tray. In time to paste a mournful expression over his angular features and cross himself as the bell in the church steeple began to toll.

"Sounds like Preacher Dibble's planting Wilkes," Billings growled as Ramon disappeared out back again. "Dirt into dirt."

Most of the sheepmen had gone out into their fields. The few laggards and the women who were on their way to the stores halted and stood with heads bowed. Glancing out onto the street and seeing this, the one-eyed man made his expression even more sour.

"Look at them!" he snarled. "Wasn't anyone except his bosom buddies and Jonas Cochran had a good word to say for Wilkes when he was alive!"

The dead man merited only ten mournful notes from the steeple bell. When the death knell ended, the sounds of Art Ely hammering metal into shape on his anvil clanged through the town.

"You're not the most talkative of men are you?" Billings complained, and raised a ringed finger toward his nose.

Edge swallowed a piece of buttered hot roll and washed it down with coffee. Then he looked at the frowning face of the one-eyed man—who suddenly realized what he was doing and pretended he had an itch on the side of his nose.

"It was you wanted to talk with me, feller. What do you want me to say about the state of your privy, and the way local folks respect the dead?"

The frown expanded. "I'm alive, sir! And accustomed to receiving respect from people I can help."

He moderated his tone. "Is money a subject that interests you?"

"It buys what I need. Fit my needs to my bankroll."

"How does a thousand dollars sound?" he laughed and it was a smirk with noise.

"Like a lot of money just to buy some respect, feller."

"One bullet," Billings said softly, his uncovered eye checking that the bead curtain hung still in the arch and that the sidewalk outside the restaurant was deserted. He leaned across the table. "You're a fine gunfighter, sir, who has already engendered bad feeling in our local sheriff. It will be a simple matter to provoke Gould into drawing against you, will it not?"

"What then, feller?" Edge asked flatly.

Billings remained in the conspiratorial attitude, smiling in anticipation of a successful deal. "I will appoint myself sheriff and Freedom will become a wide-open town."

"Just like that?"

The one-eyed man frowned again, perturbed by the half-breed's unemotional response. "Not immediately, of course. It will take time for the word to spread that Freedom no longer has a sheriff who treats every stranger like he was a carrier of yellow fever. Time, too, for me to convince the local people that my plans for Freedom will benefit all."

"And you'll be able to do all that without too much sweat just because Gould's out of the way?"

Billings had obviously expected a quick close of the deal. And now his impatience came to the surface. But he suppressed it with a long sigh. "Look, I've already got a number of the local merchants on my side. And there's a hell of a lot of ordinary people who like Four Aces style entertainment better than the liquor and spit and sawdust kind which is all Cochran offers over at the Sheepman. But in this town there's a strong strait-laced body of opinion.

59

Solidly behind Gould now. But with Gould gone they won't be any opposition at all."

Edge finished his coffee as the eagerness of the one-eyed man came to the surface again. "But all that need not concern you, sir. Because you'll be long gone. Although should you wish to return in the future—when I and my men are in control of what will undoubtedly be the most wide-open town in the territory—you will be—"

"Your men?"

Billings made a throaty sound of irritation. "Inittially Grogan and Leech. You probably saw them in the Four Aces last night. But later it will probably be necessary for me to recruit other deputies. I have no illusions about the problems involved in running the kind of town I envisage, sir. But it should not be too difficult to select the right caliber of men from those who will be attracted here." He smiled and straightened up in his chair. "The kind of man who, shall we say, will kill for such a simple reason as the fact that his horse is in need of a new set of shoes?"

"Ramon!" Edge called.

Billings was perplexed.

"Sí, señor?" the Mexican asked as he came through the bead curtain.

"How much the breakfast?"

"Thirty cents, señor."

The half-breed dug for a handful of coins and counted out the required amount. Then he stood up, hoisted the Winchester to his shoulder and stepped out on the sidewalk. There were few men on the streets of Freedom now. Just a pair of old timers killing time until they died. Several women carrying shopping baskets. And a lot of children between five and fourteen converging on the schoolhouse.

"What do you say, sir?" Billings asked anxiously as he emerged to stand beside Edge in the warm sunlight.

The half-breed nodded in the direction of the wagon parked outside the Four Aces, responding to

60

a cheerful wave from Willard Clayton who was bus-
ily engaged in setting up signs to advertise that he
was now in business as a dentist. The smile on the
face of the blond youngster was abruptly replaced by
a look of deep hatred when the boy saw Billings
emerge from the restaurant doorway. But the one-
eyed man was too intent upon staring at the impassive profile of Edge to see this.

"Well?"

The half-breed rested his rifle on a rocker to the
left of the doorway and started to take off his coat.
"Sure, I'm fine, feller," he said.

"You know what I mean!" Billings rasped. "Do
we have a deal?"

"Don't hold it against you for trying," Edge replied. "But you made a mistake. Killing ain't my
trade."

"I told you, Abi!" a man snarled. "I told you we'd
best be on our own!"

Edge had heard the footfalls on the sawdust-
strewn floor of the restaurant. But there had been no
reason to think it was anybody except Ramon. Until
the fast-spoken words were spat through the redolent
air. And the man's booted feet stomped harder.

The half-breed, his coat slid midway down his
arms, silently cursed his lack of readiness. And
cursed, too, the outwardly calm and peaceful atmosphere of this town in early morning which he had
allowed to influence his state of mind.

He whirled, trying to shrug clear of his coat and
managing only to draw his left arm free of a sleeve.

As he turned he glimpsed the face of Billings
which showed a mixture of shock, rage and fear.
Then, pressed against the rear wall of the restaurant
to one side of the bead-curtained archway he saw
Ramon, the Mexican terrified to a point close to
passing out.

Finally, the prematurely bald man with the scar on
his jaw who had emanated so much ill-will toward
the half-breed in the Four Aces last night. Dressed in

61

the same way as then, except that he had taken off the jacket of his stylishly tailored cream suit. And his eyes were no longer brooding. Instead, they blazed with green fire to complement the way his lips were drawn back from his teeth in a vicious snarl. The sun-glinting blade of the knife in his right fist was just three feet away from Edge's chest as the half-breed completed his awkward turn.

"Grogan!" Billings roared.

Edge swung his right arm forward, to whiplash his coat toward the thrusting knife. Grogan pulled up short and vented an obscenity as he tried to jerk the knife clear. He did so, but lost time. Enough time for Edge to streak his left hand into the long hair at the nape of his neck and slide out the straight razor.

"He's on his own, Edge!" Billings shrieked.

"Not for long," the half-breed hissed between teeth clenched in a killer's grin, as he dropped his coat-entangled arm to his side and pushed his right hand forward. At the same time he bent from the waist.

Grogan tried to lean backward, but his counter was slowed by the shock of seeing the blade in the taller man's fist. And Edge's longer reach, combined with the forward cant of his body, was enough for the connection to be made.

So that half the length of the sharply honed razor sank into Grogan's throat, just beneath the Adam's apple.

"Figure he'll have lots of company in hell."

Neither Grogan nor Edge had moved their feet since the half-breed completed his turn and the bald headed man halted his forward rush. So that one was still out on the sidewalk and the other was in the restaurant, the lethal thrust having been made across the threshold.

Grogan made a gurgling sound and his gritted teeth were suddenly changed from white to crimson as an outrush of air from his lungs carried blood from his punctured throat into his mouth. His eyes bulged so large it looked as if the balls were in danger of popping from the sockets. Then he dropped his knife, his mouth fell open and a torrent of blood spewed out over his chin and down onto his blue vest. His eyelids moved fractionally and he died, the downward tumble of his corpse pulling his flesh off the blade of the razor.

"Madre de Dios!" Ramon gasped, and crossed himself.

Grogan's kneecaps hit the floor hard and Edge took a backward step as the dead man sprawled half out of the restaurant doorway.

"Oh, my God!" Billings croaked.

Edge stooped down to wipe the bloodied blade on the silk back of the dead man's vest, shaking the coat sleeve free of his arm as he did so. To the corpse, he muttered, "Nobody can say you never had a prayer, feller."

Chapter Six

"SEÑOR, HE made me silent with fear when he came through my kitchen!" the trembling Ramon blurted.

"I swear I didn't know anything about what Grogan planned—" Billings said, speaking so fast his words ran together.

A woman crossing the street toward the restaurant saw the blood-run face of the dead man between Edge's booted feet, dropped her shopping basket and screamed; "Murder! Another killing!"

In the few moments it had taken for Grogan to launch his attack and for the half-breed to kill him, the morning routine of Freedom had continued on its course. Nobody on the street—except for Willard Clayton—paid the least attention to what was happening under the sidewalk awning in front of the restaurant.

But as the high-pitched words were shrieked through the hot air they triggered a period of silence that began at the suddenly immobile woman and spread outward like ripples from the center of a pond. Across and down the street, through the buildings and even out into the hilly grazing land beyond. So that not even the bleat of a sheep could be heard. A frozen scene under glaring sun.

Then: "Hold it right there, stranger!" the black-clad Huey Gould yelled, powering out of his office and coming to a halt on the sidewalk. His right hand was draped over the butt of his holstered Colt.

The silence came back. Harder and deeper than the one which had followed the shouted words of the shocked woman. As all eyes were wrenched away from the unperturbed form of the tall, lean half-breed to sweep their gazes toward the lawman. But this time the stillness was shorter lived, shattered by an awesomely loud sound. Deep-throated. Twin reports merged into one as both loads of a double-barrel shotgun sprayed through splinters of glass from the law-office window. They tore off the flesh from the back of Gould's head and sent him staggering on dead legs, down from the sidewalk and out to the street. A corpse with a shredded brain pouring out of the massive hole in his skull to splash down his back—moved by the spasms of a dying nervous system: off the patch of building shade and into the harsh glare of the sun.

The screams of horror, cries of terror and shouts of rage began before the lifeless form of the sheriff impacted against the ground to raise a cloud of dust. People fled in fear of their own lives or lunged forward to protect the youngest and most bewildered children.

"It's all right!" a man yelled from the shaded interior of the law office. "We done it, Abi! Me and Grogan, we done it without no help! You tell the people they got nothin' to fear if they just—"

He showed himself in the framework of glass shards at the shattered window. A thick-set, pale-faced, thirty-year-old man with a mop of black curly hair, thick eyebrows and eyes as blue as those of the half-breed. The man who had been seated with Grogan in the Four Aces last night. Now holding a broken-open shotgun which he snapped together as he saw Edge standing beside Billings, and made to bring it to the aim.

"No, Randy!" the one-eyed man shrieked, and stepped into the line of fire. "Enough's been done!"

"That's the feller named Leech, I guess," Edge said softly. And made no move to step from behind the shield of Billings's body. As the shocked man in the law office became as motionless as everyone else

66

who had witnessed the blasting to death of Sheriff Gould.

"I swear they cooked it up without telling me," the one-eyed man implored, with nervousness in his voice but the start of a new-born confidence in his bearing as he swung his head to left and right, surveying the effect of the recent killings on the townspeople.

"But, Abi, we got it buttoned up!" Leech yelled. "Look to the hotel!"

He set the example. Then, everyone in a position to do so shifted their gaze in the same direction. In time to see the five upper-storey front windows pushed open. So that the two whores at each of them could thrust the barrels of Winchester rifles over the sills. While, down below, Rose Pride pushed through the batwings, a similar weapon leveled from a flaring hip below her nipped-in-waist.

"It was Grogan's idea, darling!" the beautiful green-eyed blond madam called. "And we all went along with it because we were tired of waitin' for your plans to——"

"Grogan's dead, Rose!" Leech snarled. "I can see him from here!"

"I got you covered, Billings!" Jonas Cochran yelled, and pushed the barrel of a rifle through the batwings of the Sheepman. "So you tell——"

"You crazy sonofabitch!" the one-eyed man retorted, his confidence mounting by the moment. "Randy Leech and the women have clear shots at everyone on the street. Squeeze that trigger and there'll be a massacre!"

The fleshy-faced, bald-as-the-dead-Grogan saloon owner uttered a groan that augmented the frown of frustration which spread over his features.

"Same thing'll happen if you try anything foolish, sir," Billings said, lowering his voice to speak to the half-breed who stood behind him. But in the tense silence his words reached the ears of everyone who was on or around the mid-town intersection of Freedom. "You have my word—" He raised his voice again, "—everyone has my word, that there will be no further violence providing you all accept that I am now in control of this town!"

"But what about what he done to Barny Grogan, Abi?" Leech growled.

"If Grogan had confided in me, he would not be dead!" Billings snapped. Another lowering of his voice to address Edge, "What do you say?"

The northern stretch of Main and the two streets at the sides of the Four Aces were becoming crowded with people. Drawn in from the grazing pastures and out of houses and business premises by the shotgun blast and the shouting. Questions had been asked and answered and now everyone was fully aware of just how dangerous the situation was in front of the hotel.

"That I'll kill any man—or woman—who points a gun at me and doesn't use it."

For the first time since stepping in front of the half-breed, Billings turned his head to look at him. "You will not interfere with my plans for this town?"

Fear, hatred, consternation, hope, contempt, despair, eagerness and indifference were all directed toward the impassive, dark-skinned, leather-textured face of Edge which showed above Billings's shoulder. Many men in addition to Jonas Cochran had guns and were thus in positions to make a move against the Billings faction. But it was made tacitly apparent that no local man would dare to do so.

"Why would I do that now, feller?" Edge asked. And drew back his lips to show a cold grin. "For nothing? After I already turned down a part in your grand design."

As aware as everyone else that, since Cochran's play had been stopped, the outcome of the present situation depended upon what Edge did, Billings was unable to suppress a sigh and a smile of relief. Then, after the half-breed had draped his coat over one arm and picked up his rifle with his free hand, Billings turned to face the street again and became grimly determined in look and tone of voice.

"Very well, you people! I had not meant for this to happen the way it did! With killings in front of women and children! But however it has happened, I have achieved my aim! Which was to rid Freedom of the constrictions represented by Huey Gould! Now, I know I have the support of more than Randy Leech and the ladies of the Four Aces! And if the rest of you people come around to my way of thinking, this town can prosper better than if a Mother Lode was struck in the hills! And everyone will benefit by it!"

As he moved along the sidewalk of Main Street the half-breed could hear every word Billings spoke. But he listened without interest. Just as he was aware, with indifference, of the largely scornful attention which was directed at him from the townspeople who were shuffling tentatively closer to where the one-eyed man was shouting the details of his plan for Freedom, his enthusiasm growing by the moment.

By the time Edge was out where the sidewalk ended at the blacksmith's shop and livery stable, the throng was behind him. And Billings's oration reached him as an indistinct droning sound.

Both the big doors were open and the heat from the forge fire was harsher than that of the eight o'clock sun. The mare was still in the stall and Edge paid scant attention to the set of shiny shoes which lay on the anvil as he crossed to take down his saddle and bedroll from the hook beside the stall. He had lashed his coat to the roll by the time footfalls ceased to sound out on the street and Art Ely's frame cast a long shadow across the floor.

"If you got plans to leave town on that mare, you're gonna have to change them, mister," the blacksmith growled.

Edge slid the Winchester into the boot, straightened up and turned around. He pointed a long, brown-skinned finger at the shoes on the anvil.

"They made for my horse?"

"Yeah."

"Guess I can fit them myself."

A nod. "I reckon you can do that, mister. If you got the same regard for a dumb animal as you do for your fellow men. Your mare's got thrush comin' on both hind hooves."

Edge grimaced and turned back to the stall. He lifted the latch and opened the half door. Even as he dropped onto his haunches he knew Ely had spoken the truth. For, despite the other strong smells in the stable, the stench of infection from the animal's inner hooves reached his nostrils. Speaking soft words of reassurance and gently running a hand over the animal's thigh, he raised first one hoof and then the other. And his grimace deepened into the lines of his lean face as he saw the pus-filled areas on both frogs which were giving off the sickening odor.

"Town got a veterinarian, feller?" he asked as he came erect and closed the stall.

A nod. "Sherman Hayes. But he went south awhile ago. Expected back on the stage this mornin'. I've cleaned up the frogs and I'll keep them clean until Sherman gets here. But I reckon it'll be a number of days before you can ride that animal again. She's a real fine horse, no mistake. Must've been painin' her a time."

Edge knew it and could understand why a man like Ely, who worked with horses, was finding it hard to conceal his resentment.

"Sure," the half-breed muttered, remembering briefly how he had been so preoccupied for so long with the simple pleasures of having a horse to ride under the enormous sky after the constriction of New York City. Then, all vagueness gone, "It's a good horse. Will be again when she's fit. I'm willing to trade for any animal that is fit."

He raked his slitted eyes over the other six stalls that were occupied.

"Two of them are mine and I ain't doin' no tra-

70

din'!" Ely said grimly. "Another pair's the kid's who come into town ahead of you last night. You can ask Jonas Cochran about the black geldin'. Or Busby Tuttle if he'll do a swap with his piebald mare. But the way things are shapin' in this town, mister, I don't reckon anybody'll want to be stuck with a lame horse."

"Obliged for the information about the stage coming through this morning, feller," Edge said, stooping to lift his gear.

"What about your horse?" Ely asked, dismay in his voice and expression as the half-breed came toward him.

"Figure I'm leaving the animal in good hands."

"I don't want nothin' from you, mister!" Ely snapped as Edge stepped out onto the sunlit street. Which was still crowded with people on the intersection in front of the Four Aces. But there were no guns in menacing sight now. And no one was shouting. Instead, there was a low-keyed, disconsolate murmur as the citizens of Freedom stood in small groups, discussing the violence of the morning and its implications.

"Then have this Hayes feller shoot her when he gets back to town," the half-breed replied evenly as he started back up the street.

The elderly blacksmith hurried to get alongside Edge and the two of them were level as they stepped up onto the sidewalk.

"Figure that's your way with everythin' you got no more use for, mister. Get rid of it. Everythin' and everybody."

"Ain't never been one for collecting junk," Edge allowed, his voice still evenly pitched in contrast with his blatant disdain.

And Ely realized his attitude was leaving the half-breed untouched. "There's junk and junk," he muttered. "And the sort we got runnin' this town now is the trash sort."

"So get rid of it, feller."

Ely spat into the street and then pressed his top teeth hard against his lower gums. "Just like that, uh?"

Edge pursed his lips as he came to a halt in front of the stage-line depot and telegraph office. And nodded to the many small groups of anxiously whispering people on the intersection. "There's a whole bunch of fellers with guns in the crowd. Just needs one of them to draw and kill Billings. Same way one of his boys blasted Gould. Well-known fact that if you cut off the head of a sidewinder, you got nothing to fear from his rattle."

"Easy to say," Ely growled.

"And do," Edge answered, shifting his narrow-eyed gaze to the still open window above the entrance of the Four Aces. Where the one-eyed Billings stood, smiling wistfully as he peered out over the people below him, absently raking slime from his left nostril. A piece at a time, which he rolled between his thumb and forefinger, then flicked off to the right, daydreaming of the future and totally oblivious to the present.

"What?" the blacksmith asked, puzzled. Then saw the direction of the half-breed's inscrutable gaze and looked up at the window himself.

Edge smiled coldly. "Easy as Abi see."

Chapter Seven

"YOU CAN shoe a horse, but you ain't no good at makin' the shoes, mister," Art Ely growled. "Like me and a lot of men in this town could draw a gun— but we couldn't kill anybody." His dark, weak and wary looking eyes found the half-breed's lean face and then moved quickly away. "And I ain't sayin' we can't aim straight, you know what I mean?"

"I know what you mean, Mr. Ely," Willard Clayton put in as he emerged onto the threshold of the stage-line depot, the grimness in his face and voice seeming to age him far beyond his immature years. "And it could just be that you won't have to worry about Billings for very much longer, sir."

Jamie used to look much older than he was when he had a powerful emotion gnawing at his insides.

"Easy kid," Edge drawled. "You need more than hate for a man to kill him. If he can see you coming."

"Go on about your business, you people!" Billings shouted down from the hotel window as he finished mining in his nose and emerged from his reverie. "And think about the kind of men who've decided to see things my way."

Inside the hotel barroom, Rose Pride shouted an order and the Negro musician began to thump out a familiar tune on his piano keyboard.

The crowd started to disperse from the intersection. But even before this happened, certain aspects of life in Freedom had recommenced. The bodies of Huey Gould and Barny Grogan had been carried

73

along First Street to the undertaking parlor. The children had been hurried to their schoolhouse. Randy Leech had discarded the shotgun and now stood in the open doorway of the law office, his hands draped over the jutting butts of a pair of matching Frontier Colts, wearing a five-pointed star on his vest front and a proprietorial grin on his face.

"I'm takin' it easy, Mr. Edge," the youngster answered tensely. "Until Abbie gets here I ain't even sure I'm aimin' my hate at the right man. If I am, then I'll start to worry about how straight I can shoot."

"What the hell you talkin' about boy?" Ely asked, his tone and attitude lacking in interest as he saw a man beckoning to him from the street.

The man was the chin-whiskered gunsmith who had been in a group with the bug-eyed Tuttle and four other men who had the look of merchants rather than sheep raisers. The rest had moved into the Sheepman Saloon and it was obvious that the gunsmith was eager for Ely to join them.

"Nothin'," Clayton answered quickly, and seemed to regret what he had said—thoughts spoken aloud which should have remained secret.

"And that's just what you're gonna do, boy!" the blacksmith said sternly. "We don't want no wet-behind-the-ears kid gettin' himself killed on our account!"

Anger flared across the youthful features of Clayton. He seemed ready to yell a retort at Ely, but shot a glance across the broad street at the grinning Leech and rasped with controlled fury, "You attend to your affairs and I'll take care of my own!"

The blacksmith replied in an identical tone before he swung down from the sidewalk and stalked across the street. "I don't know what business you're talkin' about, boy! But bear this in mind— any innocent folks get hurt as a result of what you do, you'll wind up fuel in my forge!"

74

"He expect me to take that threat seriously?" Clayton muttered. "Gutless old fool."

"Most fellers'll do what they say if they're fired up enough kid," the half-breed drawled, shifting his slitted eyes from the bulky frame of Ely to the short and skinny youngster in the doorway. "If you don't take him seriously, could just be you'll end up as light relief."

Clayton seemed on the point of pursuing the subject in the same tone as before. But then he shrugged his slim shoulders. "You got time for a cup of coffee, Mr. Edge?"

"I got until stage time."

The boy grinned. "I just checked. Due in at 10:30. With a thirty-minute turnaround. Appreciate some advice."

"Don't do it," Edge said, moving along the sidewalk and turning in through the restaurant doorway.

Ramon was on his way to the bead-curtained arch, carrying a mop and a pail. He had washed Grogan's blood off the floor and scattered fresh sawdust over the wet patch. The much larger splash of crimson had been left to congeal into a brown crust on the street in front of the law office; an awesome reminder to the citizens of Freedom that a cold-blooded killer now wore the five pointed star in their town.

"Two coffees," the half-breed told the Mexican, who looked at him and broke out in a sweat.

"*Si señor,*" Ramon replied hoarsely, and pushed quickly through the strings of beads.

"Don't do what?" Clayton demanded anxiously.

Edge dropped his gear to the floor and sat in the same chair he had occupied earlier. What was left of the breakfast he shared with Billings had been cleared from the table. As the boy lowered himself into the chair the one-eyed man had used, the half-breed answered, "Try to kill Billings."

The youthful features became set in a grim expression. "I got to. If he's the one."

75

Edge raised his shoulders a fraction of an inch. "No sweat, kid. Advice costs nothing. Never is any obligation to take it."

"You don't know the full story."

"But I figure I'm going to hear it."

Now the youngster became sullen. "If you ain't even willin' to listen to—"

Edge shook his head. "I got the time to spare and you're paying for the coffee, kid. And I never take anything for nothing."

Ramon re-entered the restaurant with the order and the abruptly eager Clayton had difficulty in containing himself until the nervous Mexican had withdrawn into the back. The place was as filthy as before, but the appetizing smells of baking bread, cooking chili and brewing coffee continued to permeate the hot atmosphere. And Edge found it easy to be reminded of the kitchen of the Iowa farmhouse on long ago Mondays—his mother's baking days. Jamie had never liked chili, which had been a favorite of his father and older brother.

"It was fifteen years ago," Willard Clayton said, his voice low, pulling a part of the half-breed's mind back from a more distant past. "Just before the start of the war. I was only four years old. Abbie was fourteen. We used to travel with Pa. All over. Wherever he went with his magic show. It was in St. Louis Pa was shot down by a man with only one eye. At a poker game. The one-eyed man was cheatin' and when Pa accused him, he pulled a gun and shot him. But we was strangers there and the one-eyed man, he had a lot of friends. And it was told to the law that Pa was the one that was the cheat."

The boy paused and watched as Edge licked the gummed strip of a cigarette paper then struck a match.

"Seem to recall that last evening you told me your father spent years teaching you how to do magic tricks, kid," the half-breed pointed out.

Clayton looked pained. "In a way, he did. He used

76

to invent new things all the time and write them down in a big ledger. When he was murdered, I wasn't old enough to understand what was goin' on. And nobody told me nothin' except that Pa had died. Abbie and me, we was sent to our Pa's sister in Atlanta. But Abbie, she run away and what with the war gettin' started, nobody could find her. She found me, though. After the Yankees burned Atlanta and Aunt Esme was killed. She came for me and took me to New Orleans, where she worked in a dancehall."

As he unfolded the story, Willard Clayton's face showed an increasingly embittered expression; his mind obviously recalling more recent menories in stark detail.

"I lived with her there until two years ago, Mr. Edge. And I went to school and in my spare time I learned all Pa's tricks. Then Abbie told me how Pa had been murdered and she took me to St. Louis to show me his grave in Potter's Field. And I knew then I had to find the man who killed him and make him pay. Which was what Abbie wanted, too. And not only because we needed to take revenge for Pa being killed and branded a card cheat. Apart from that, the one-eyed man had caused Abbie to end up a dancehall girl. And I'd spent six miserable years with an aunt I hated and I never had the college education Pa had always planned for me."

Clayton broke off again, and stared intently through the drifting tobacco smoke at the unresponsive face of Edge. "One life ended and two more ruined," the boy rasped. "A man who caused that, he deserves what's comin' to him, I reckon."

Across at the Four Aces, the piano player was taking a break. There was still noise in the hotel barroom, but it was all low key. So that the regular thuds of spades biting into earth as two more graves were dug could be clearly heard.

"Men have died for a lot less, kid," the half-breed allowed.

Clayton grunted his satisfaction with this. "We

didn't have much to go on. It had happened thirteen years before and there had been a war since then. But it seemed like a good omen when we found Pa's old wagon rottin' in a warehouse. So we done it up and tried to find out more than Abbie already knew about the man who killed Pa. But we didn't have no luck and we started out to look for him only knowin' he was one-eyed and called himself Jack Smith. Except that Abbie had seen him once so knew what he looked like a long time ago."

"Two years," Edge said.

"What?"

"You and your sister have been tracking him for the best part of two years?"

A grim-faced nod. "Yeah. At first we traveled together, but then we realized we could cover more ground by splittin' up. And what with me doin' my magic shows and bein' a dentist, and Abbie workin' as a . . . dancer, we could afford to keep ourselves while we moved about."

There were people on the street again. Both men and women. Attired in mourning and shuffling slowly across the intersection and onto First. People who for the most part wore expressions of grief and misery, but some spared brief baleful looks for the law office and the Four Aces as they headed toward the church.

"How many one-eyed men you turned up, Willard?" Edge asked.

"Billings is the third," the youngster answered, suddenly disillusioned. "Abbie's found four I know about. Maybe more, but she don't have to telegraph or write me every time she thinks she may have found Pa's killer. On account she knows what he looks like. What with the war and all, lots of men got wounded and—"

"Your sister and you ain't never far apart; her being able to get a stage to Freedom this soon?"

"We was lucky this time, Mr. Edge. I was pullin' teeth up in Tonopath when I heard about the one-

78

eyed man who operated the hotel here in Freedom. And Abbie happened to be workin' a saloon down in Lathrop Wells. I gave a miner down on his luck twenty-five dollars to ride to Lathrop and tell Abbie to meet me here. There was a telegraph from her when I arrived last night. Sayin' she'd be on the mornin' stage. And I got a feelin' that this time we got the right man."

The bell in the church steeple began to toll the death knell. And the mourners who were late for the funeral of Huey Gould hurried to get to the graveyard. Somebody in the Four Aces shouted drunkenly and the piano player began to thump out the up-tempo melody of "Down Yonder." The group of businessmen who had adjourned to the Sheepman did not leave the saloon to see the former sheriff of their town put into the ground.

"At the wrong time, kid."

The boy licked his lips as he listened to the church bell tolling in competition with the piano music and glanced out across the deserted, brightly sunlit street to where Leech continued to stand in the doorway of the law office.

"That's what I need your advice about, Mr. Edge," he said nervously. "If Billin's is the man who killed my Pa, he's the only one I want to see dead. Though I'm willin' to kill anybody who tries to stop me. But I don't want no innocent folks to suffer. And I ain't gonna do it sneaky, though. I ain't gonna shoot him in the back nor nothin' like that. On account of that would make me no better than he is. I want it to be face to face and man to man. With him knowin' why he's gettin' it and who it is that's makin' him pay."

Edge drank the last of the coffee.

"If you was me in this town today, what would you do?" the youngster pressed.

"I'd wait for the stage to reach town—"

"I mean, if Abbie says Billin's is the man," Clayton cut in impatiently.

Edge nodded. "Then I'd just walk up to the feller—get real close if I shot a gun as badly as you after two years of practice—and I'd kill him."

"I've only been shootin' a couple of months. Before that I was too fired up about findin' the man who killed Pa to think about how I'd get my revenge."

"No difference, kid. All you asked was what I'd do if I was you. Told you."

"But I ain't never seen Billin's with a gun. And Leech and the other men that have sided with him—they might start blastin' at me soon as I'd killed Billin's. Which could maybe start the whole town to . . . everyone shootin' at everyone else."

"Seems I misunderstood you, kid," Edge said with a sigh as he leaned down, picked up his gear and got to his feet. "Figured you wanted to get even with somebody in your past. I've done that. More than once. So figure I'm qualified to give advice on it. Never been much of a hand at planning for the future."

He went only as far as the rocker out on the sidewalk, where he settled down with his gear on the boarding beside him, the saddle placed so that the stock of the Winchester jutting from the boot was close at hand.

Across the street, Leech glowered at him and then withdrew into the deep shade of the law office.

Willard Clayton jingled some coins on to the table and then emerged from the restaurant. For a moment, he hesitated and seemed ready to continue with the subject. But only grimaced and vented a low grunt of frustration before he stepped down from the sidewalk and walked purposefully across the intersection to mount the steps and enter the Four Aces. He was not this morning wearing the gunbelt with the Tranter in the belly holster.

Enthusiastic bellows of greeting filled the barroom as the batwings swung closed behind the youngster.

"If he follows your advice, he will most surely die, *señor*," Ramon said sadly as he came to a halt on the threshold of his restaurant.

"Doing what he wants to do, feller," Edge answered flatly. "Best way to go."

"To live is better," the Mexican said, pulling closed the door of his restaurant and turning a key in the lock.

"You weren't listening hard enough, Ramon," the half-breed drawled, as the black-clad townspeople began to return from the burial. "The kid was talking of death."

"To an expert. It is a subject with which you are most familiar, *señor*."

"I been close to it a few times," Edge allowed wryly.

"We are all close to it now, I think. I must tell the men meeting in the saloon of what the boy plans to do."

"Are you not open today, Señor Alvarez?" the gray-haired Widow Emmons called as she approached the Mexican's premises, a basket in her hand. "I must have some bread."

"Later, *Señora*," he replied as he set off to cross the street. "There is other, more pressing business I must attend to first."

The woman halted and fanned a hand in front of her sweat-beaded face. Then gave a snort of disgust when she saw the Mexican push through the batwing doors of the Sheepman.

"Drunkards and cowards all!" she said bitterly, and shared her scorn among the somberly dressed men who had attended the funeral. "We lost the only man worthy of the name when Huey Gould was shot down!"

Some of the men pretended not to hear her taunt and hurried away. Others who were ready to take issue with the woman were urged by their wives to quicken their pace.

81

Martha Emmons shook her head and looked at the half-breed who sat totally at ease in the rocker. "And to think that last night I was tryin' to win your sympathy for these spineless sonsofbitches and their yellow womenfolk!"

"Sheep raisers and storekeepers, ma'am," Edge said flatly. "Family men most of them. Or old men. If any of them were fighters once, the easy years you told me about have softened them."

"What?" she blurted, her round and pale face becoming spread again with an expression of bitter scorn. But she had heard what he said. "So they had some easy years? All the more reason they oughta be ready to fight to keep things the way they were! Why, if I were a man . . ."

She let the sentence hang unfinished in the hot, bright air and her whole being bristled with the anger and frustration as she turned to glare at the façade of the Four Aces.

"You wouldn't have anything to get off your chest and it would be a whole new ball game, ma'am," Edge said into the pause she had left.

She returned her attention to him, the set of her features unchanged. "And Art told me you accused Huey Gould of bein' all smart mouth, mister!"

"He had an interest in this town. I don't."

A sigh blew the froth off her anger. "How much would it cost me to buy your interest, Mr. Edge?" she asked.

Edge rasped the back of his brown-skinned hand over the bristles on his jaw. "Billings tried a thousand, ma'am. But the way it turned out the sheriff died for no charge. Could be you'll get what you want for nothing."

She was intrigued and perplexed. But another man spoke before the half-breed could respond to Martha Emmons's quizzical look.

"Hey, Billings! Billings, can you hear me?"

The raucous words were shouted by the broad-shouldered, fleshy-faced, bald-headed Jonas Cochran. Who stood on the sidewalk in front of the saloon's batwing doors. He was unarmed.

Not so Randy Leech, who stepped across the threshold of the law office with a Winchester held two-handed with the hammer back.

All the mourners had left the street by now and, as the noise from the Four Aces subsided and then stilled, the Widow Emmons scuttled up on to the sidewalk to stand beside Edge.

"You got somethin' to say?" the curly-headed Leech snarled.

"Not to you, you murderin' bastard!"

Leech made to bring his rifle to the aim, his features forming into a murderous glower.

"Hold it, Randy!" the one-eyed man snapped. As he pushed open the batwings of the hotel entrance and stepped out. Flanked by Lee and Travis who each draped a hand over the butt of his holstered revolver.

"We had a meeting of the town council," Cochran called across the intersection to Billings who had adopted an expression and pose of receptiveness. "Of them councilmen who ain't thrown in with you, anyway."

"And?" Billings was smoking, the rings on his fingers sparkling in the sunlight in competition with his watch chain as he raised and lowered his right hand.

"We don't want no more killin' in Freedom!"

"I think you will have no trouble getting that decision endorsed, Jonas."

"Shuddup and listen!"

Billings's expression hardened and Leech, Lee and Travis all came close to swinging their guns to the aim.

"We're doin' you a friggin' favor, damnit! And we want it returned. That young guy who does the magic tricks, he's fixin' to kill you an—"

83

"The hell you say!" Billings croaked, and snapped his head around to peer into the barroom.

"I ain't through yet!" Cochran yelled as the two men flanking Billings also swung to seek out Willard Clayton. "Favor we want is for you to let him outta your place unharmed!"

Billings was not listening. He was rasping low-voiced instructions to Lee and Travis. And even over the distance of the broad intersection, Edge could see the sweat of fear standing out on the profile of the one-eyed man.

Edge drew his Remington and Martha Emmons gasped as she saw the move and heard the hammer click back and the further clicks of the cylinder turning. Then she vented a short laugh. And Billings choked on a sudden surge of greater fear as the gunshot cracked; the bullet kicked up fragments of cement a fraction of an inch from his highly polished left shoe.

By the time all eyes had raked across the dusty street and located Edge, the hammer of the revolver was back again and a fresh shell was in front of it.

"You missed!" the stoutly built woman beside the half-breed accused.

"Nobody move!" Edge yelled. And unfolded his tall, lean frame from the rocker. The creak of the chair's ancient timber provided the only sound until Edge spoke again, his tone less urgent. "Except the kid. He moves out of there."

"Abi, I can take him!" Randy Leech snarled.

Billings's lips moved, but no words emerged.

"Don't reckon your boss wants to trade his own life for the stranger's," Jonas Cochran said, abruptly almost cheerful in contrast to his former demeanor.

"Abi, the kid's runnin' for the rear door!" Rose Pride called shrilly.

"Let him go!" Billings answered, his voice coming close to the same pitch as that of the woman as he succeeded in undamming the fear which had closed

84

his throat. Then he managed to tear his single eye away from the muzzle of the leveled Remington and stare into the impassive face of Edge. "You? The kid? I don't understand none of this, Edge!" The words were no longer shrill. Instead, his tone was a thick croak.

"Me neither," Martha Emmons growled. Then she caught her breath. "The kid . . . ? He was what you meant when you—"

"Okay, Mr. Edge!" Willard Clayton shouted as he sprinted from the rear of the Four Aces, across First Street and into the cover of a barn on the other side of an alley from Ramon Alvarez's premises. "I'm out!"

"Tell your men to put away their guns, feller," Edge called to Billings.

"Do like he says!" the one-eyed man ordered, the worst of his fear past. Then, after Leech and Lee and Travis had grudgingly complied with the command, "But I warn you, mister! You got until stage time! If you and that punk kid ain't headin' out of town then, I'm declarin' open season on you!" As Edge eased the Remington hammer forward and holstered the gun, Billings's good eye raked across the street to locate Cochran. "And you and the rest of them no-account do-gooders been talkin' up a storm, you're wastin' your friggin' time! I'm runnin' this town now and I got all the men that matter on my side! And anyone don't do like we say, there'll be open season on them too! Like it or leave it! Stay and cause trouble and you'll wind up like pigeons at a shoot!"

He spun around and pushed hard through the batwings. The grim-faced Lee and Travis moved after him more slowly, backstepping into the Four Aces with their eyes fixed upon Edge and their hands draped over their gun butts.

"Pigeons hell!" Martha Emmons growled as she surveyed the empty streets of Freedom with a cold-eyed glare and heard the murmur of anxious voices

85

from the Sheepman after Cochran had re-entered the saloon. "Doves more like. All they want is peace and quiet."

"Whichever, I guess they understood the word from Billings," the half-breed replied as he lowered himself into the comfortable rocker again. "Coup."

Chapter Eight

"GEE, THANKS a million, Mr. Edge," Willard Clayton called from the doorway of the stage-line depot. "You saved my life."

"Makes us even, kid," the half-breed replied as a new sound vibrated in the hot morning air. Reaching town from the south—the rattle and hoofbeats of the approaching stage. More than an hour ahead of schedule. Heard over a distance because there were no loud competing sounds from the hotel and the saloon and the houses, just a constant low murmur of urgent talk.

"I never—"

"No, you didn't," Edge cut in on the youngster's puzzled response. "Because you didn't practice enough. You were a lousy shot last night and you haven't had the time to improve."

Clayton stepped out onto the sidewalk, the tension in his features being displaced by a broad grin as he heard the sound of the stage running in off the open trail and onto First Street. He was now wearing his gunbelt with the belly holster.

"Hey, it's early." His expression clouded. "I sure hope Abbie didn't miss it."

"What's goin' on here?" Martha Emmons demanded. "What's your quarrel with Billin's, son? Why'd those spineless bastards over at the Sheepman warn that one-eyed sonofabitch about you?"

"What's maybe between me and Billin's is personal, lady," Clayton said, his face clouding with a frown again as he shifted his gaze away from where

87

the stage would show on the intersection and looked hard at Edge. "How did Cochran know about it, sir?"

"The Mexican, kid. He heard what you told me and he was worried about you. Don't know how Cochran and the others feel about you. But I figure most of them were scared about you missing another shot and innocent people getting gunned down by men who know their business."

The sounds from the stage became less frenetic as the driver slowed his team for the final run up along First Street and across the intersection.

"My, my, my," a man with a reedy voice announced as he came out of the stage-line office, staring down at a silver-cased watch in his palm. "It ain't never been this early before."

His build and features were a match for his voice. He was short and skinny and had a narrow face which was emphasized by the over-sized eye-glasses he wore. He was about fifty and looked like a man who might wither away to nothing if he stayed too long in the sun. Unlike everyone else who watched the stage come to a dust-raising halt at the side of the street, he showed not the least sign of having been affected by the morning's events in Freedom.

The arrival of the stage, presaging as it did its eventual departure and the reaching of the truce deadline set by Billings, attracted the tense attention of everyone else who was in a position to watch. Covertly or from out in the open. While the depot clerk was solely concerned with his job.

"Mornin' Bart!" he called to the bearded driver through the stirred up dust. "You been tryin' to set some kinda record? I sure hope you didn't give the passengers too rough a ride."

"It's the most hair-raising trip I've ever taken, Jake!" a man said, pushing open the door and stepping down onto the sidewalk. A broad-shouldered, barrel-chested, square-faced man of middle years who coughed on some dust and smudged some more across his forehead as he mopped at his sweat with a kerchief.

Jake looked worried. "Sorry, Mr. Hayes, but—"

The town vet waved a hand and grinned. As he turned to help a second passenger down from the stage. "Who could refuse such a lovely young lady anything, though," he said. "It would have been much more pleasant for me if the journey had taken twice as long."

The veteran driver of the stage spat over the street side of his seat and started to hand down baggage to the clerk. "She said double fare if I'd clip an hour off the run, Jake," he growled. "Mr. Hayes, he said he didn't mind. And the company, they don't have to know about the extra, do they?"

Abbie Clayton was as fine a looking woman as Hayes had said. This was clear to see, even though she was as ravaged by the effects of long, fast, grueling travel as he.

She was about thirty, close to six feet tall and yet had a body which made her look almost petite. Her blond hair fell to her shoulders in a series of elegant waves, framing an oval face which had a flawless complexion. Her eyes were the lightest blue and she had very red, full lips. There were lines in her skin, but they served to add maturity and character to what would otherwise have been mere empty beauty. She wore a wide-brimmed red hat trimmed with white lace and a low necklined dress of the same colors—tight fitting around her upper body and arms and flaring dramatically from her narrow waist.

To Edge, who had heard from Willard that his sister worked in dancehalls, she looked like a high-priced whore. But, he realized, with a stab of cold anger in the pit of his belly—the emotion triggered by the association with his first impression—she also looked like something else. Somebody else. Which was perhaps something he should have expected, since Willard bore a resemblance at certain times to Jamie. Abbie Clayton reminded Edge of his long dead mother.

"You don't know her, kid!" the half-breed rasped as he came up out of the rocker. And moved quickly toward the woman.

"What?" Willard blurted.

"You crazy or something?" Abbie snapped, her bright smile dropped in favor of a frown that was half angry and half puzzled.

"I beg your pardon, sir?" Hayes blustered.

Even Bart and Jake were distracted from their unloading chore by the perplexity Edge had caused.

"Listen to the man!" Martha Emmons rasped. "We got trouble here. And so far this is the only man who's done more than talk about it." The driver, Hayes and Abbie dragged their gazes away from Edge to look to left and right. The Widow Emmons added wryly, "Though not much."

"What kinda trouble, Jake?" Bart wanted to know.

"Hell, the streets sure are empty for this time of day," Hayes put in.

"Willard?" Abbie asked anxiously.

"Huey Gould's dead," Jake said. "So's Barny Grogan. Chris Wilkes got it last night. Billin's has taken over Freedom. Made Randy Leech sheriff. Got some of the local big wheels seein' things his way."

"Billin's could be our man, sis," Willard urged. "I figure we got nothin' to lose by playin' this the way Mr. Edge wants it."

The woman swallowed hard. "Act like we're not brother and sister? I don't know if I could—"

"Sure you can, lady," the half-breed put in, taking her arm and steering her across the sidewalk to the locked doors of the restaurant. "I just saw you come off the stage."

Chapter Nine

THE LOCKED door of Ramon Alvarez's premises burst inward with a crash of splintering wood as Edge's boot heel hit it.

"Buy you a cup of coffee and tell you all about it," the half-breed said as the woman tried to come to a sudden halt on the threshold. He could still smell her perfume despite the cooking aromas which filled the place.

"Trust him, sis, he just saved my life!" Willard augmented.

"What you do to my place, *señor*?" the Mexican yelled as he ran across the street.

Other, heavier footfalls sounded. Less hurried.

"Whose side are you on?" Martha Emmons hissed as Ramon came around the front of the sweat-lathered horses in the stage traces. Then glowered at the rifle-toting Leech who appeared at the rear of the Concord.

The newly appointed sheriff ignored the woman to gaze at the shattered door, the couple on the threshold and then at the angry and anxious Alvarez.

"Damage to private property," he proclaimed. "You want to press charges, Mex?"

Edge appeared at ease, but during the stretched second Ramon hesitated, his muscles bunched and his mind raced behind the cold, unblinking blueness of his slitted eyes. His rifle was out of reach and his right hand was clutching Abbie's upper arm. Leech was far out of range of the razor. And he knew the man with eyes as blue as his own and the same disre-

91

gard for human life would react violently if he got the answer he wanted from the Mexican.

"It would seem there has been an accident, *señor*," Ramon said at length. "Perhaps it was not realized my door was locked."

Leech vented a grunt of frustration. Then, "Bart, you get this rig ready to roll as soon as you can. We got a stranger here who ain't welcome."

"Sure thing, Randy," the bearded driver acknowledged. "But the team'll have to be rested awhile."

"Not too long," Leech said and turned his head to nod to the sweating veterinarian. "Mr. Hayes. Guess you'll be told by the Mex and the Widow Emmons what's happened in town today. You want to throw in with Mr. Billin's, you'll be welcome over to the Four Aces. They'll likely tell it different, but Mr. Billin's wants things run peaceable—soon as the troublemakers are run outta Freedom."

Now he raised a hand away from his Winchester to touch the front of his mop of hair as he looked admiringly at Abbie. "And if you're lookin' for work, there'll be plenty over at the hotel once the word gets around."

He spun on his heels and swaggered back across the street. Then, in response to a call from Billings, he changed direction and forsook the law office for the Four Aces.

Abbie Clayton wrenched herself free of Edge's grasp. "Word about what?" she demanded. "Will somebody tell me what this is all about?"

She allowed herself to be steered through the doorway and to a table by her brother, who began to talk excitedly about his belief that Billings was the one-eyed man for whom they had been searching for almost two years.

Hayes, the Widow Emmons and Ramon also entered the restaurant, listening intently to the fast-spoken words of the boy but having their curiosity satisfied only to an extent when Willard began to outline the violent events of the morning.

Edge remained on the threshold but turned his back on the anxious group as he rolled and lit a cigarette. And then, while he smoked it slowly, he watched the town come to life again, restarting the daily routine which had been earlier curtailed by gunfire and sudden death.

Few of the townspeople still wore mourning, but there was a funereal quality in the way they moved about their business; many of·them casting surreptitious glances toward the hotel and the restaurant. Soon after the first of the women had appeared with shopping baskets and the sheepmen had begun to ride or trudge out toward the pastureland spread over the hills around Freedom, Art Ely led the exodus from the saloon. Behind him were the bug-eyed Tuttle who crossed to his drugstore down the street beyond the stage-line depot, the bewhiskered man who did not need to cross over to reach the premises where he sold guns and shells, a fat-gutted old man who entered the dry goods store and then another man who looked like he might be the most prosperous sheep farmer in the area.

The bank remained closed. As did a row of stores on the street which forked to the southeast side of the hotel. Feed and grain, a butchery, the barbershop, a hardware merchants and a drapers. Beyond these was a long, single storey building which had several signs jutting from its roof. The *Freedom Weekly News* was housed in the building. Also a land agent. Edge could not read the more distant signs. There seemed to be little activity in the premises beneath the signs.

But, he thought as he raked his glinting, slitted eyes over the scene, if Abi Billings proved to be the wrong man, the whole town could be back to normal in a few days—even hours. For it was just an ordinary town filled with a broad cross-section of ordinary people. Decent people, most of them, who had struggled hard in the early days of their town to build it and to achieve whatever ambitions they had individually aimed for. And now they had it—had been enjoying the fruits of their labors for the easy years Edge and Martha Emmons had spoken of.

Would the lives of these ordinary people alter to any great degree if Billings was allowed to become entrenched in his position of power? Back in Iowa, the Hedges family—the mother as beautifully blond and blue-eyed as the dancehall girl in the restaurant—had lived their daily lives unaffected by the power struggles of local, county, state and national office.

Most people did, willingly sacrificing principles or simply lacking interest in events they considered beyond their control. Until somebody who felt more strongly made a stand and demanded or forced others into a commitment. And when that happened and the comfortable peace was shattered by gunfire who could say with authority, after the cost was counted, that it would not have been better to compromise?

Be it to prevent a war fought to keep one nation from splitting into two. Or to condone the taking over by violence of a dull sheep-farming community in order to change it into a wide-open mecca of vice and gambling.

"Very well, Mr. Edge," Abbie Clayton announced. "We are all now familiar with what happened this morning."

"And with the reason for this couple's interest in Billin's," the Widow Emmons added.

"So maybe you'd tell us why Abbie and me gotta make out we ain't brother and sister, sir," Willard said.

"You may trust me," Sherman Hayes assured. "And count on any help I'm able to give. I have absolutely no intention of taking up Leech's invitation to join forces with the Four Aces crowd."

"Be awhile," the half-breed answered, dropping his cigarette end to the sidewalk and crushing it out under a boot heel. "Like for Ely the blacksmith to hear what I have to say."

The group in the restaurant spoke words and showed expressions of impatience. But Edge had already moved out of the doorway, to saunter north along Main Street. As he went past the window and entrance of the stage-line depot, he glanced inside. There were four women in front of the counter, waiting eagerly for the reedy-voiced Jake to sort through the contents of the mailbag which was one of the items unloaded from the stage. The bearded Bart was nowhere to be seen, although he had left his rig and team to go into the office with Jake as soon as the unloading chore was finished.

Edge had to walk on beyond Tuttle's drugstore before he was able to make a left turn into an alley beside the fire station, where he halted to check if anybody was watching him.

Leech was still in the Four Aces, which was again filled with the noise of people celebrating victory.

Shopping women and storekeepers were for the most part busy trading.

Only the short, pot-bellied man with red sideburns and chin whiskers was having a slow day in his gunsmith's store. And it was obvious he had been watching the progress of the half-breed—from the way he suddenly and nervously turned his back on the street and hurried into the shadowed depths of his premises when the slitted eyes of Edge located him.

The back lots of the premises on the western side of Main Street were littered with crushed cardboard cartons, broken open crates and weathered items of merchandise which had been discarded for one reason or another. Beyond the strip of dumping ground there was a rutted track which gave access to storage shacks and, in the case of the fire station and the stage-line depot, stables. In back of these buildings there was a barbed-wire fence which kept the sheep from wandering off the grazing land and into town. Up on the hillside which rose gently away from the fencing, a group of men were engaged in replenishing a number of water troughs.

95

As far as he was able to judge, Edge reached the rear of Ramon Alvarez's premises without being seen by the sheepmen. The rear door through which Grogan had apparently gained entry earlier that morning was not only unlocked, it was ajar. The smells which came out through the crack between door and frame were stronger and more appetizing than those which filtered into the restaurant. This was because, the half-breed discovered as he eased open the door wider and stepped through, Remington drawn and cocked, he was closer to their source. For the door gave directly onto the kitchen and bakehouse.

Immediately opposite—beyond a large table with a row of big ovens on one side and two over-sized ranges on the other—was a second doorway, its door also ajar. He could not hear voices until he was at the door. Then only as a distant murmuring, coming from beyond the archway with the bead curtain at the end of a fifteen-feet-long hallway with closed doors to either side.

The man who stood tensely in the hallway, close to the bead curtain, was hearing every word clearly. It was the bearded Bart, who had shown no sign that he was pretending a friendliness he did not feel when Randy Leech spoke to him. And who had directed several less than friendly glances toward Edge while the half-breed stood in the restaurant doorway and he was unloading the stage freight.

"*Dispense usted,*" Ramon Alvarez said. "I must take the bread from the—"

Bart vented a low grunt and turned, grimacing at the effort to move silently. Then fear displaced mere anxiety as he saw the tall, lean, gun-toting form of Edge framed in the doorway.

"I . . ." he croaked.

"*Como se llama?*" Ramon gasped as he parted the strands of beads, saw the broad back of the stage driver.

"I come to throw in with you people," Bart

96

blurted. "The back way 'cause I didn't want the Billin's bunch to see me."

He remained rooted to the spot as Edge advanced along the hallway. Then screwed his head around when he heard a disturbance on the other side of the archway. The scrape of boots on the sawdust strewn floor and a cry of alarm from the Mexican.

Than a hand chopped hard through the beads, its straight edge cracking heavily into the side of Bart's neck. The man groaned and crumpled to the floor like a loosely packed sack of potatoes. The sweating features of the square-faced Sherman Hayes were pushed through the beads. They were formed into an expression of satisfaction.

"Most humane way to put down rabbits and such like," he said. "Never tried it on a man before. Sure hope I didn't kill him."

"You put him to sleep is all," Edge answered as he stepped over the raggedly breathing man. "The kind he'll wake from."

"He was lyin', Edge," Martha Emmons said.

"If I had been sure of that, I would have acted quicker than Señor Hayes," Ramon claimed, trying hard to sound convincing.

"You're as big a liar as he is," the grim-faced woman accused. "You know as well as everyone else in Freedom that Bart Briggs spends every spare cent he has on whorin' at the Four Aces whenever he's in town!"

The Mexican was crestfallen. "Is true," he admitted. "I am a coward."

"But you can make yourself useful," Hayes pointed out. "Take care of Briggs so he won't be able to pass on to Billings what it was he overheard."

"Si, señor," Ramon agreed with an eager-to-please smile. "This will be well done."

"Like your bread, feller," Edge drawled.

The Mexican wrinkled his nostrils and then struck his forehead with the heel of a hand. "Dios mio!" he

97

exclaimed as he ran between Edge and Hayes and lunged through the bead curtain, leaping over the unconscious form of Briggs.

Edge pushed the Remington into its holster and glanced around the hard-set features of Sherman Hayes, Martha Emmons and the Clayton brother and sister before he scanned the sections of street visible through the open doorway and greasy windows of the restaurant. "Seems," he drawled, "there's something in this town that ain't half-baked."

Chapter Ten

"YOU'RE NOT so damn hot!" Abbie Clayton snarled, and in anger looked nothing at all like the woman from whom Edge had inherited his ice-blue eyes. "Telling Willard to just walk up to Billings in his own hotel and shoot him! With God knows how many kill-crazy men like that monster Leech looking on!"

"Sis, I wouldn't have been stupid enough to just do it like that and not—"

"Be quiet, Willard!" Abbie snapped. "You seem to think this man saved your life. Seems to me he almost got you killed. It was Ramon who—"

Her brother was sullen, "I wouldn't have done nothin' until you got here and said Billin's was the man."

Martha Emmons stamped her foot. "All this is beside the point." She glared at Abbie and Willard and then expanded the expression as she directed her attention to the half-breed. "We ain't even half-baked, mister. Because we got nothin' at all cookin'. On account of we're waitin' for you to finish what you started when the stage reached town."

"It certainly appeared to me that an idea crossed your mind," Hayes augmented.

"That wouldn't have taken long," Abbie growled.

"You be quiet, Abigail!" Willard told his sister.

Edge looked from the Claytons to the older couple and then lowered himself into the seat at the table he had occupied twice already today. "I told the kid what he asked. What I'd do if I was him. Don't know how good Billings's guns are, but even if they're the best there are, it was sound advice. Putting myself in his shoes and that means I'd be a lousy shot."

"Mr. Edge—" Martha Emmons started to interrupt.

"Let the man finish, my dear," Art Ely said as he turned in off the sidewalk. "If he figures he has the time to talk, we oughta have the time to listen." The blacksmith nodded to the veterinarian. "Sherman— good to have you back in town."

"Carry on, Mr. Edge," Willard urged.

"Best gunslinger in the world doesn't fear the second best," the half-breed continued as Ely dropped into another chair at this table. "It's the worst that worries him, on account of he's likely to be unpredictable."

"Words," Abbie growled. "Adding up to an excuse. You've said them now. But you still haven't explained why Willard and me need to pretend we're not related."

"I reckon that's clear enough to see, young lady," Ely countered. "Billin's knows this town and everyone who lives here. He knew that once he'd got rid of Huey Gould there wouldn't be anyone with the wits and guts to whip up a stand against him. And that was how it happened. It was . . . how's that word, mister? Predictable, ain't that right? Only chance we got is to spring a few surprises on that bunch at the Four Aces."

"Willard and me aren't here to fight your battles for you!" Abbie protested vehemently.

"Just to start the war," Edge answered.

"That's right, sis," her brother said before she could rebut the half-breed's comment. "If Billin's is the man who killed Pa and I blast him, all hell is gonna break loose."

There was a break in the talk and everyone except Edge looked expectantly at Abbie. The half-breed continued to watch the Four Aces as customers began to leave, as eager as most other citizens of Freedom to get back to normal now that their positions had been established. Merchants and professional men, glowing with the effects of liquor and doubtless feeling they had a properous future ahead of them, providing their merchandise and services for a far greater volume of passing trade.

Out beyond the bead curtain, Ramon could be heard dragging the unconscious Briggs along the hallway and into the kitchen.

"We don't even know if he is the right man yet," Abbie said at length. "And if it turns out he is, then we can bide our time. We've waited years, so we can wait a little longer."

"No, Abigail," Willard corrected. "The stage is due to leave Freedom at eleven. If me and Mr. Edge ain't out of town by then, Billin's is gonna send his men for us."

"And that won't be no surprise, miss," Ely added.

Another pause, but this time it did not last so long.

"Very well," Abbie murmured tautly. "What do you have in mind, Edge?"

"A drink, lady. Over at the Four Aces."

"You're crazy," Ely snapped.

"For me to take a close look at this man Billings?"

"Yeah."

"And see you get gunned down?"

"Don't figure that'll happen. So far Billings has played it straight. He says Grogan and Leech started the killing without his knowledge and I believe him."

"Why, for God's sake?" Martha Emmons asked.

"Because he doesn't want a town run by gunlaw, ma'am. The kind of people I've just seen coming out of his place look much like you and Ely and Hayes and Tuttle."

"Hamilton Janson from the bank," the blacksmith muttered bitterly. "Joe Wilde who runs the newspaper. Dekes our land agent and Frank Rollin's who takes care of all the legal work around town. Them and a few more who was always behind Billin's in

101

tryin' to make Freedom into somethin' it never oughta be."

"Back-stabbin' bastards, all of them!" the Widow Emmons spat.

"But not many of them I'd guess," Edge said, "who'd take much more killing and still stick with Billings. Because men like that will know that if Freedom gets known as a town where the gun settles all differences, the high-spending trade will stay clear."

"After you took that shot at him, that one-eyed nose-picker sure didn't sound like a man who wanted peace," Ely growled.

"He made a promise is all," the half-breed allowed. "To send his guns after the kid and me, if we were in town after the stage time and to kill any townspeople who cause trouble. Seems to me he was on safe ground in threatening the local citizens, most of who don't have any intention of getting in his way. And I'm ready to take the chance that he'll hold off trying to get rid of the kid and me until the deadline's reached. If for no other reason than to prove to his business buddies that his word's to be trusted."

"All right," Abbie said suddenly, moving toward the front of the restaurant. "I'll go over to the hotel with you."

"Why you ready to take that risk?" Ely asked as Edge rose from his chair.

"It's no risk," Abbie answered. "This Billings guy doesn't know me."

"I'm talkin' to Edge, lady," the blacksmith said, and there was suspicion in his eyes as he gazed up at the tall, lean half-breed. "Not so long ago, you didn't give that for what was happening in this town."

He snapped his fingers.

"A while ago I hadn't been threatened," Edge answered flatly. "Guess there's a lot of towns all over where I ain't welcome. Don't want there ever to be another one where I'm this much unwelcome."

"What about me, Mr. Edge?" Willard asked anxiously.

"Stay out of sight, kid. Billings knows you've got an axe to grind. My head doesn't go on the block until eleven."

"It's almost ten now," Ely warned.

On the threshold of the restaurant, Edge made to take Abbie Clayton's arm. But she flinched clear of him.

"Be safer for everyone if you pretend to like me, lady," he told her and moved out onto the sidewalk.

"Come on, sis," Willard rasped. "For Pa."

The woman stepped quickly outside to catch up with Edge and pasted a smile across her lovely face as she linked her arm through his.

"Play acting is all," she said in a tone that was no match for the smile she wore. "Like me not being Willard's sister."

"No sweat," he said as they stepped down from the sidewalk and started across the intersection toward the hotel.

The appearance of Edge on the street and the direction in which he escorted the woman drew countless pairs of nervous and even shocked eyes toward him. Conversations in normal tones were interrupted, then quickly restarted on a different subject and with the words low and rasping.

The half-breed ignored everyone and everything on the streets and in the stores to survey, with apparent casual indifference, the façade of the Four Aces.

"Willard told you I work the dancehalls?" Abbie asked, her voice now in line with the smile.

"That's right."

"But I never work for anyone except me when it comes to closing time, mister. Which means I can pick and choose."

"Fine," he responded, and generated a smile of his own, which drew the lips back from his teeth but failed to reach the heavily hooded eyes which glinted from the shade of his hat brim.

103

"I saw I sparked something in you when I got off the stage. Only fair to tell you that if it was me made you change your mind about the situation here, you don't have a chance of getting to first base."

"No sweat," he said again. And, as he turned his head briefly away from her smiling face, he murmured, "Be like incest."

"I like what I do, Edge. And when I'm not too pushed for eating money, I'm not against selling what I have for whatever a man says he can afford. If I *like* the man."

"I got your message, lady," he said as they passed Willard's wagon and started up the broad steps toward the hotel stoop. "And here's mine. If you saw a spark, it didn't set nothing alight. I'm not like so many of the men in this town."

"You've lost me."

"No matter how you spell it out, lady, I don't want a piece at any price."

Chapter Eleven

NOBODY IN the Four Aces had watched the couple advance across the intersection, so there was genuine shock when Edge pushed open the batwing doors and escorted Abbie Clayton into the barroom.

Sam, the Negro piano player, was the first to see the half-breed. And he snatched his hands off the keyboard as if music were a sin and Edge an avenging angel. The abrupt cessation of the familiar "Down Yonder" caused everyone already in the barroom to look at Sam. Then they immediately swept their gazes toward the doorway on which the Negro's enlarged eyes were fixed.

Billings, Leech, Lee and Travis were in a close-knit group at a center point of the bar. Rose Pride and four of her whores were playing poker with no stakes at a corner table. Three whores sat at tables with potential clients. Another whore was midway down the stairs, just ahead of a satisfied customer. The two Negro bartenders.

"What the frig, mister?" Randy Leech snarled, and swung his body in the same direction his head was facing, at the same time reaching down for the Winchester which rested against the bar.

"Hold it!" Billings ordered, through teeth clenched to a cheroot. And in part of a second his look of shock was changed to a smile of admiration as his one eye took in the sight of the beautiful face and provocative figure of the woman beside the half-breed. "Miss, you'd likely have been the best thing I laid eyes upon on the best of days. But today . . ."

He allowed the sentence to hang unfinished. Then hardened his tone and expression to snap, "You said you didn't drink before noon, Edge."

"But today . . . is exceptional," the half-breed replied wryly. "So I'll make an exception."

"You're wise, Edge," Billings said, his tone easing. "It's a long, hot stage ride to Dry Springs. And there they only have water to slake a man's thirst."

Abbie Clayton continued to display her acting skills. Neither by a flicker of an eyelash nor the merest tensing of her body did she reveal disappointment that Billings was the wrong man, or evil delight that he was the right one.

"They got beer and liquor over to the Sheepman, mister," Leech rasped and his expression showed that he was almost tasting the frustration of not being allowed to touch his rifle.

While Lee and Travis, who seemed as drunk as they were last night when Chris Wilkes stirred up the trouble, directed an even deeper brand of hatred toward the half-breed.

"Hey, now," Billings said lightly. "The good times aren't rolling quite yet, Randy. We mustn't turn away business to the competition."

"Funny business, I bet," the sheriff muttered.

"Don't you think you'd better return to your duties?" Billings told him, injecting a note of authority into his voice. "It would seem to me that this is the least likely place in town to require the presence of a peace officer."

He glanced casually but pointedly around the barroom. And like trained animals, Lee and Travis straightened their backbones and flexed their muscles. While the man with the whore on the stairs and the three who sat with girls at tables moved fractionally to display the revolvers in their gunbelt holsters. And the two Negro bartenders bellied close to the counter and hooked their hands over the top, signaling that there were guns of some kind within easy reach.

106

All the men worked some degree of hardness into their eyes as they looked briefly toward the half-breed. The whores cast appraising surveys over Abbie Clayton, and Rose Pride tried to generate a sneer of contempt that lacked conviction—seemed concerned only with the brightness of the smiles which had been exchanged by the tall blond on Edge's arm and the one-eyed man.

"What'll I do, Abi?" Leech wanted to know.

Billings ground out his cheroot under a boot heel and drew his lips into a taut line for a moment. Then rasped: "I don't know, Randy! Get the window of the law office fixed. And—oh, yes—tell Bart Briggs to get the lead out. He brought the stage in early, so there's no reason why he has to wait until eleven to get rolling again."

Leech was less tense when he felt the weight of the Winchester in his hands.

"Play us some music," Billings said to the man at the piano. "And what is your pleasure, sir?" he directed at Edge. "In the way of a drink, of course. It would seem you are already catered for in another service we provide at the Four Aces."

Edge steered the woman directly from the doorway to the bar, forcing Leech to move to the side on his way out. Sam began to play "Greensleeves." Lee and Travis backed off to the end of the bar at the foot of the stairs and the man who had been to the room with the whore went out of the hotel. Low-voiced conversations got underway again. As did the poker game with no stakes, the madam surrendering her hand to the whore who had just turned a trick. Rose Pride went to the end of the bar near the piano player and called loudly for a bottle of rye and a glass.

"Beer," Edge told the closest bartender and looked at Abbie as the woman disengaged her arm from his.

"I never touch alcohol of any kind," she responded.

107

The Negro shrugged and went to draw the half-breed's beer. Billings's uncovered eye brightened and made a close-up survey of the woman's features and upper body.

"There are only two other reasons a lady would come to the Four Aces, Miss . . . ?"

"Smith," Abbie supplied and Edge looked hard into the images of the woman and the one-eyed man reflected by the mirror behind the bottle and glass-lined shelves. Smith was the name the killer of her father had used all those years ago in St. Louis. Neither reflected face showed any telling reaction to the name. "Abigail Smith."

"To gamble or to . . ."

"I know a heart from a diamond is about all. And I can see those stones in your rings are real, Mr. Billings."

The one-eyed man laughed as Edge exchanged some coins for the glass of beer the Negro set down in front of him.

"Randy said he mentioned work to you, Abigail. And he certainly did not exaggerate when he told me what you looked like. Just as I am not exaggerating when I tell you there will be no shortage of work—and money to buy trinkets like these," he waved both his many-ringed hands in front of her. "—now that I am running this town."

"What I heard, Mr. Billings."

"Call me Abi, Abigail."

Edge had achieved what he set out to do in coming into the Four Aces. Which was to discover how much firepower Billings commanded, and estimate the quality of it.

Leech, Lee and Travis he knew about, of course. These three all around thirty. Young enough and capable of handling themselves in a dangerous situation. With good reason to hate the half-breed—and anyone he allied himself with—after the ways in which Wilkes and Grogan had died. Leech from a city background, like Billings. Lee and Travis a cou-

108

ple of Western drifters. The trio of useful men to
have on your side in a fight—provided they had
somebody to give them orders and the promised re-
ward at the end of it was high enough.

The three men drinking with whores were of a
kind with Lee and Travis. With the look of saddle-
tramps who rode from one town to another, one
spread to the next, hiring out whatever skills they
possessed to pay for eating, drinking and screwing.
Cowpunching, fence mending, sheep shearing and
general handyman skills, the half-breed guessed. Not
one of them had the stamp of a professional gunfighter.

The man who had left the barroom after descend-
ing the stairway from the upper floor of the Four
Aces had looked like a clerk or a storekeeper. How
many of his kind would back Billings if it came to a
showdown with guns deciding the issue? Few of
them, he decided. Certainly all of them had got clear
of the hotel long before the stage was scheduled to
leave Freedom.

The Negro bartenders and the piano player? They
were working for a Southerner with aristocratic pre-
tensions. They would do as they were told.

And that was the opposition. A bunch of men like
Billy Seward, Bob Rhett, John Scott, Hal Douglas
and Roger Bell. Not a Frank Forrest among them.
Which could turn out to be a bad omen for the re-
spectable people of the town of Freedom. For if Billings was the man the Clayton brother and sister were
after, and the kid got lucky and killed him, there
would be nobody with authority to take command.
And with nothing to gain from surrender, men like
Leech and Travis and Lee might well elect to vent
their spite against the town.

Whereas in the war, on the occasions when Captain Josiah C. Hedges was unable to give the orders—like the time he caught a bullet and was unconscious for a long period—Sergeant Forrest had
adequately filled the breech.

Edge vented a low grunt of self-anger.

"You say something, sir?" Billings asked.

"Not a thing," the half-breed replied and finished his beer. He was angry at himself for allowing his mind to bring back memories of the distant past in an attempt to draw parallels with the present. To justify why he should have allowed himself to be mixed up with the troubles of Freedom and the murderous ambition of Willard and Abbie Clayton . . . Which meant he was reaching for the material to build a false premise.

None of the men Billings had gathered about him were anything like the vicious bunch of troopers the half-breed had commanded during the war. Willard only very remotely resembled Jamie. And his blue-eyed blond sister was a part-time whore which had to rule out any parallel between her and the clean-living woman who had died so long ago in Iowa.

So, Edge was involved because his fate had decreed he should be. And, as always in such a situation, he had known from the start that he was fighting a losing battle in trying to remain neutral. A battle against destiny and his own intrinsic nature.

For he was the only born killer in town. Unless Billings . . . ?

"This beautiful young lady has agreed to give Freedom a try," the one-eyed man said. "While you have been deep in thought. And I am willing to pay more than a penny if you have been reconsidering—"

"Be leaving soon, feller."

Billings became earnest. "A man has to settle someplace sometimes, Mr. Edge. I used to travel all over in the old days. San Francisco, Denver, New Orleans, St. Louis, Chicago, El Paso, San Antone—"

"Doing what, Abi?" Abbie Clayton asked.

Edge met her eyes in the mirror and just for part of a second she revealed that she knew the answer to the question she posed.

"Playing cards, mostly." He smiled with satisfaction. "Reason for the name of this hotel. It was a hand of four aces that won me the bundle I used to build it with. Off a cattle baron in Abilene."

He abruptly became aware of the fact that Lee and Travis had curtailed their own talk and were listening to him—and were as suspicious of him as of Edge.

"You guys want to step outside and have Art Ely hitch that Clayton kid's team to his wagon. The kid's probably too scared to do it himself, this close to the hotel."

They moved grudgingly to the door, shooting sidelong glances at the two men and a woman standing midway along the bar. After they had left, the batwings flapping behind them, Billings lowered his voice to talk fast.

"Listen, Edge. This town has potential. I saw that from the start. It was a dull town then. Still is, I guess. But before the Four Aces was built, all it had by way of entertainment was that crumby place Jonas Cochran runs and church socials. And you know what that meant? You've looked around. It's full of middle-aged couples and old timers. No young people, because they up and leave soon as they start flexing their muscles.

"That's no good for a town. You heard what happened to Huey Gould's young wife. And how Emmylou lit out almost soon as the wedding cake was eaten. Lot of other youngsters did the same thing. Boys and girls who wanted more than mutton every meal and bad liquor served in dirty glasses over at the Sheepman."

"I'd want more than that," Abbie said when Billings left a pause and Edge showed no inclination to fill it.

"So does everyone," the one-eyed man continued, his enthusiasm unabated. "Even the people who live here, as they'll soon realize when Freedom gets put on the map. I bear you no grudge, sir. I don't blame

111

you for turning down my offer. The gun's not my way anymore. I don't even carry one now.

"But Huey Gould had to be got rid of, Edge. He was an old-style lawman running an old-style town and for as long as he wore a badge in Freedom the place was held back.

"Well, he's out of the way now and you seen already that I've got the local men that matter on my side."

He broke off again, and this time used the mirror to check over the people who he did not want to hear what he was saying. Of them, only Rose Pride was showing any interest in the trio at the bar. And her malevolence was obviously concentrated on Abbie Clayton.

"What I haven't got is a replacement for Gould who I can rely on, sir. And I'm going to need one. Because Freedom is bound to draw in all kinds of people. The good and the bad. The ones who come to enjoy themselves and those who are looking for trouble. And I don't want this to be a Dodge or a Newton or an Abilene or any of them Kansas cow towns. And to keep it from being that, I'll need a lawman as hard and tough as Gould was. But with a different way of looking at things. And I reckon that you'd do that job better than Randy Leech, Lee and Travis all rolled into one."

He was through now. Signaled this by the way he sighed, poured a whisky from the bottle he had been sharing with the men he held in such low esteem, and knocked it back at a swallow. Then fixed the intent gaze of his good eye on the bristled face of the half-breed.

"No deal, feller. Like before."

Billings's hand folded around the empty shot-glass, shook. Then an angry frown took command of his face. Which perhaps meant the shakiness of his hand was not caused by anger.

"Then get out of my place and out of my town, sir!"

112

"And take your woman with you, mister!" Rose Pride snarled.

"The hell you say!" Billings snapped, wrenching his head around to look at her.

She came down the bar toward him, having to lean against the counter to keep from staggering. She held an empty glass in her right hand and the half-empty bottle of rye in the left. Her eyes were glazed with the effect of drinking.

"Sure I do! I'm madam at the Four Aces. And I pick the whores." She stared with contempt at Abbie. "We're all filled up."

"You are!" Billings told her, his voice a hiss. "With whisky!"

His anger with her became mixed with that he felt for Edge and he lashed out with an arm. The blow was a back-handed slap which cracked viciously against her cheek, the rings on his fingers dragging the skin and opening up three bloodied ruts.

Rose screamed her pain and staggered backward for three short, awkward paces. Then fell heavily to the floor, the glass and bottle breaking. Sam curtailed his piano playing and many of the watchers gasped.

"You shit!" the madam shrieked from the floor after she had drawn a hand over her cheek and looked at the blood on her fingers.

"Not as one of the girls," Billings said to Abbie. "The position of madam has just become available."

"You shit and bastard!"

"What do you say, my dear?" the one-eyed man posed, calm and collected again, as he totally ignored the enraged woman sprawled on the floor amid broken glass and spilled liquor.

Abbie smiled. "I'd be a fool to turn down a bed of Rose's, wouldn't I?"

"A wise choice, my dear. I'm sure you will be very happy here in Freedom."

Abbie's smile was more radiant than ever. "I have

113

a feeling this is going to be the happiest day of my life," she said, turning away from the bar.

Edge also swung toward the doorway.

"Where are you going?" Billings asked.

"To get my valise from the stage depot."

"I'll have somebody get that for you."

"Let the bag get her own baggage!" Rose Pride snarled as she finally managed to get to her feet.

"I'll do it myself," Abbie insisted, and fell in beside Edge on the way to the batwings.

"You want more!" Billings roared and Edge and Abigail Clayton heard more gasps, another sound of flesh on flesh, then the scream and thump as the drunken madam was again knocked to the floor. "How much more you want?"

"No darling! Please! I love you! I don't want any other woman—"

"Shut up, bitch!"

"What's goin' on in there?" Leech demanded as he reached the top of the steps and found his view into the barroom blocked by the forms of Edge and Abbie who emerged from the batwings.

"The madam just took a pratfall, sheriff," the woman replied.

Edge added, "Matter of injured Pride."

Chapter Twelve

"You?" LEECH snarled. "You caused trouble again, mister?"

"Don't point that rifle at me!" Edge rasped.

But the muzzle of the Winchester was aimed at his belly over a range of four feet before he had finished the warning.

"I got him, Abi!" Leech yelled, his teeth fully displayed in a grin of triumph.

Lee and Travis had just completed fixing Willard Clayton's team into the wagon traces. And they were alone on the otherwise deserted stretch of street which ran north from the front of the Four Aces. In one of the stores on the eastern side of the street a clock sounded a single chime to mark the time of 10:30. A half hour short of when the stage was scheduled to leave. But it was obvious that Randy Leech had made it known that Billings was not prepared to abide by the schedule. So, aware that the deadline might be reached at any moment, the peace-loving citizens of Freedom had once again withdrawn to the safety of their homes and business premises.

"I can blast him to hell!" Leech added, his voice rising.

The footfalls of the one-eyed man sounded on the floorboards in the bar room. As Edge stood, tense with controlled anger and fear behind his outer veneer of relaxed casualness. Only the utter coldness of his slitted eyes—like blue threads through the lashes—offering a clue of the lengths he was pre-

115

pared to go to survive. To put Abbie Clayton's life on the line, if necessary, by pushing her in front of the menacing rifle as he hurled himself back against the batwings.

"I will not work for a man who breaks his word!" the woman said coldly, just as Billings came to a halt.

The sigh of the one-eyed man reflected disappointment.

"Rose brought the trouble on herself," he said. "Let the man pass, Randy."

Lee and Travis allowed their hands to drop away from their holstered Colts.

"All this word-of-honor stuff is crazy," Leech hissed, and spat out of the side of his mouth as he shifted the Winchester to hold it across the front of his belly.

"Don't say thanks," Abbie whispered after Edge had steered her around the angry and tense Leech and down to the foot of the steps.

"Didn't plan to."

"How's a man get to be so mean as you, mister?" It was a rhetorical question, spoken as a rasped insult.

"Takes a lot of experience."

They veered to the left and started toward the front of the restaurant, where the door was still open to admit the bright sunlight of mid-morning. But nobody could be seen inside.

"Hurry back, Abigail!" Billings called, and hardened his tone to, address the half-breed. "And you get right on the stage, sir. Travis, roll that wagon over to the side, in case Clayton isn't so trusting as—"

"Abi, what I got to tell you!" Leech blurted. "Bart Briggs ain't no place around and nobody'll say—"

"Run!" Edge yelled. And released his hold on the woman's arm to shove her hard in the small of the back.

116

They had reached a point midway between the foot of the hotel steps and the doorway of the restaurant.

Abbie took several more steps at an involuntary run, her breathing curtailed by the shock of the half-breed's sudden switch from brooding to violent action. Then speeded her steps as Edge whirled, drew his Remington and sent a shot toward the hotel entrance. At the same time as her brother shrieked, "Sis!" and showed himself in the restaurant doorway to trigger a bullet from his Tranter.

Edge aimed for Leech, but in the final fraction of a second before he fired he tilted the gun—as the sheriff raced around behind Billings to plunge into the safety of the Four Aces. And the bullet chipped stone off the front of the hotel and ricocheted into the ground inside the parked wagon.

Willard's shot kicked up dirt and raised dust close by.

Both of them near to where Lee and Travis stood, half-crouched in reaction to the sudden flurry of action.

Billings, a look of terror etched deep into his face beneath his slicked-down hair, voiced his emotion and whirled to plunge into the barroom behind Leech.

This as the two horse team, spooked by the gunfire, reared and lunged into a gallop. Dragging the wagon in their wake, its wheels locked by the brake blocks. Dust from beneath the rims and the pounding hooves of the horses billowed up around Travis and Lee.

Edge triggered two more shots into the ground at the foot of the hotel steps, then whirled and took long strides toward the restaurant—leaping up on to the sidewalk and snatching his Winchester from the boot as he raced past his heap of gear and made it into the cover beyond the doorway.

Lee and Travis were late in getting started on their sprint for the safety of solid walls, lunging from out of the billowing dust cloud, scrambling up the steps and smashing through the batwings.

The half-breed had slid his Colt into the holster, pumped the action of the Winchester and reached a position where he could have got off a shot, before the two men went from sight.

"You could've blasted one of them!" Martha Emmons accused.

"And killed Billings at the start of it," Art Ely said, his tone much calmer.

"I'm half-Mexican and I don't like having a gun aimed at me when I told somebody not to do it," Edge replied evenly.

A fusillade of shots exploded from the Four Aces and he folded himself flat against the wall between the open doorway and the greasy window. To look impassively at the group who suddenly flung themselves back beyond the bead curtain as bullets and shards of glass cracked and showered across the tables, chairs and sawdust covered floor.

"Riddles we got no time for!" Martha Emmons yelled.

And the final two words of her response reached far out into the suddenly silent town. For, just as the opening gunshots had set the horses to panic, so the volley of fire from the hotel brought them to a sudden halt. Outside the dry goods store, the animals exhausted by the effort of dragging the dead weight of the wheel-locked wagon.

The better-schooled team in the stage traces continued to stand patiently where Bart Briggs had stopped them, recovering from their frantic race into Freedom.

"Leech called Ramon a Mex like it's a dirty word," Edge said flatly, resting his rifle against the wall while he turned the cylinder of the Remington. "He also pointed a gun at me twice."

He extracted the spent shellcases from the chambers of the revolver and took fresh bullets from his gunbelt, carefully inserting them to load the gun fully again.

The silence outside lengthened, seeming to stretch time and yet, strangely, to contract it, so that countless pairs of eyes which peered fearfully at the street registered the shortening of shadows as the sun rose higher in the cloudless sky.

Edge slid the Remington back into his holster and picked up the Winchester. He used the rifle to reach across the opening and hook the door closed.

A single shot cracked out of the hotel and the bullet slanted into the timber of the sidewalk in front of the restaurant door.

"Hold your fire, I said!" Billings shrieked.

"So Leech is the only feller that bothers me," the half-breed drawled as footfalls sounded in the hallway and the Widow Emmons came out through the bead curtain. Followed by Willard, Art Ely, Sherman Hayes, Abbie and then Ramon Alvarez. "Couldn't get a clear shot at him."

"Billings, sis?" Willard asked tensely, his fingers white from the tight grip he had on the wooden butt plates of his Tranter. "He the one?"

"Yes, he's the one right enough," the woman replied tautly. "I'm certain of that."

The boy drew himself up to his full height and set his lips in a thin line as he thrust the Tranter into his belly holster. "Then he's a dead man."

Now that doubt had been removed, all the youngster's apprehension drained out of him and there was not a single crack visible in his resolve to do what he felt he had to do. For several moments, everyone in the restaurant—in which the former cooking smells were now only faded memories clinging to the stained walls—was aware of the boy's depthless determination.

"Billings doesn't carry a gun, kid," Edge said, the soft-spoken words drawing all attention back to him, As he spoke, he recalled the way the ringed hand of

119

the one-eyed man had shook as it held an empty shot glass.

"But he's surrounded by men who do, Willard," Abbie added anxiously, and as she looked at her brother it was as if all his nervousness had been transferred to her.

"Nine if you count the piano player," Edge supplied. "If there are none upstairs. Plus the whores who had Winchesters awhile ago."

"The only ones in town, Edge," Ely growled. "Phil Webb who owns the gunsmith store, told us over at the Sheepman earlier that last night Grogan and Leech bought up all his stock of repeaters."

"Damn him for not warnin' us!" Martha Emmons snapped.

Ely grimaced, but Sherman Hayes spoke the words.

"Hell, we all know Webb," he growled. "He's for Billings's ideas and he'd be over at the Four Aces now if he had the guts to fire any of them guns he sells."

"Many more share his ideas but have the courage of their convictions?" Edge asked, spending more time peering out from the side of the shattered window than he did looking at the group who stood or sat at the rear of the restaurant.

"Hard to tell," Ely answered.

"One feller with a gun in his belt left Billings's place while I was over there. Way the hotel is placed, a whole bunch of men could sneak in through the rear door."

"My opinion you ain't got nothin' to worry about there," the Widow Emmons said bitterly. "All of them who want that nose-pickin' sonofabitch to win will be fence-sittin'. Same as decent citizens who'd like to see Billin's rottin' in hell." She altered from her sneering tone to add, "Present company excepted, of course."

"We're ready and willing, that's for sure," Hayes

120

allowed morosely. "But what can we do? There's only Edge and the boy armed."

"Until now, Freedom hasn't been the kind of town where anyone needed to carry a gun," Ely muttered in the same tone.

"Webb'll still have some revolvers in his store?" Edge asked.

"I reckon," Ely said, brightening.

"How about the law office?"

Gloom clouded the blacksmith's face again, and he spoke through his upper teeth clenched to his lower gums. "Huey carried a revolver and just kept the shotgun and a Winchester in his place. Leech has got the rifle."

"Cochran's got a repeater, Art!" Hayes reminded.

"I'm with you people!"

The shouted words broke the silence which was clamped over the town. Then the pause which followed was shattered by the blast of a double-barrelled shotgun.

Edge saw a window to the right of the Four Aces entrance shatter into a million fragments. Then chanced making himself a bigger target by leaning further across the broken window of the restaurant to catch a glimpse of the bald-headed Jonas Cochran just before the saloon keeper stepped back from the batwings of the Sheepman.

Then the half-breed ducked into cover himself, as a burst of rifle fire splintered timber and smashed glass in the façade of the saloon.

"I always hated that loud mouth, but suddenly I love him," Sherman Hayes said gleefully.

"He's killed Sam, Abi!" a man in the Four Aces yelled.

"And I always hated those damn tunes that nigger played over and over all the damn time," Martha Emmons growled.

"Seems time's gone by for him," Edge murmured wryly. "Sam won't ever play anything again."

121

"The time, it passes for all of us," Ramon said anxiously as the sound of angry voices faded inside the Four Aces. "Should not somebody do something? But not in my place, maybe? For I am with you and it is not good the restaurant should be broken up."

"He's right about one thing," Martha Emmons snapped. "We gotta do more than just wait around in here for that Billin's bunch to come and get us. If we can't see anybody goin' into the hotel we can't see anyone comin' out either."

"I'll go watch out the rear door," Hayes offered.

"That's no good!" Willard told him. "We gotta do somethin' positive." He hitched up his gunbelt and it immediately fell back to where it had been before. "How'd it be if I called him out? Billin's? Settled it on a man-to-man shootin'?"

"No, Willard!" Abbie snarled, then eyed the half-breed with grudging admiration. "Your first idea worked pretty well, Edge. You got any more?"

The tall, lean, bristle-jawed man at the side of the window was directing the unblinking gaze of his slitted blue eyes to an area of sloping pasture visible in back of and above the law office.

"One," he answered.

"If it'll work, one's all we need," Art Ely said with enthusiasm.

"Spit it out, son," the Widow Emmons urged. "You can count on us."

"Long as you don't count on my idea," Edge said with his lips curling back from his teeth in an ice-cold grin. "I don't want anyone outside of the Four Aces to be caught napping."

"Another friggin' riddle!" the older of the two women in the restaurant snarled.

"What d'you have in mind, mister?" Hayes asked.

Edge shifted his gaze from the grazing meadow to the front of the hotel and said, "Sheep."

Chapter Thirteen

"YOU PEOPLE in Alvarez's place! And everyone else who can hear what I'm sayin'! Includin' you, Cochran! Mr. Billin's is willin' to give Freedom one last chance! Killin' can be all over if you all listen and do like you're told! So you listen and you listen good!"

Perhaps five minutes had crawled into history since Martha Emmons and Abigail Clayton were left alone in the restaurant and bakery. Although the older woman, who stood at the kitchen and bakehouse doorway with Edge's cocked Remington in a fist was not strictly alone. For the tightly gagged Bart Briggs was spreadeagled on the big table, his wrists and ankles lashed to the tops of the legs. Abbie stood against the wall between the door and broken window in the restaurant, holding her brother's Tranter in both hands against her chest as she listened to Randy Leech's shouted words. The metal barrel of the revolver became greasy with the sweat that oozed from her pores and ran towards the valley between her breasts.

She knew that Willard would be sweating, too. And Ely, Hayes and Ramon. Edge, as well. Though the impassive half-breed's pores would be opened by exertion, not fear, she thought. Willard had the furthest to go. Out of the rear of this place, along the back lots of the buildings on the west side of First, across the street, over the street that forked to the left of the Four Aces and then turn to come back northward. His first stop would be at the Sheepman to warn Cochran of what was planned. Then the two of them would go to Webb's premises for handguns and shells.

Her brother had been assigned to undertake this part of the plan because he was the youngest and fittest. He also happened to be the smallest. So there was less of a chance of Willard being spotted by anxiously watching eyes in the Four Aces as he ran from one area of cover to the next.

Once at the gunsmith's store, his part in Edge's scheme was only partially completed. He then had to get the revolvers and ammunition back to where the half-breed, the Mexican, the blacksmith and the veterinarian waited; none of them sheepmen but three of whom had spent a long time in a sheep raising community and all four familiar with handling animals.

By the time Leech had finished calling attention to the Four Aces, and Billings began to deliver yet another ultimatum, Abbie Clayton had neither seen nor heard any sign of her brother. And she prayed that this was a good sign. Then added another prayer that the one-eyed man should make a long speech.

"This is stupid!" Billings yelled from one side of the batwings. "Stupid, senseless waste of human lives! Chris Wilkes, Grogan, Sheriff Gould, Sam Jordan—and Bart Briggs as far as I know! And to what end? The man called Edge began the trouble here. And for some reason known only to himself, the boy I hired to provide some much needed entertainment in this town wants to kill me! Jonas Cochran has allied himself with these two strangers! Why Jonas? Your business stands to gain as much as anyone else's when people start comin' to Freedom!

"Same goes for your boardin' house, Martha! And Ramon Alvarez, I figure you wouldn't be with these people except it was your bad luck they chose to hole up in your place!

"And, Art! Art Ely! Unless I've missed my guess, you're puttin' your life on the line only because of what happened when Wilkes pulled a gun on you!

"Sherman Hayes—well, it's the same with you as the Mexican, isn't it? You had the bad luck to step down off the stage right into the middle of this mess! And you, Miss Smith, you're in there against your will! I know that!"

He paused to catch his breath.

"You all through, Billin's?" Cochran yelled.

And Abbie breathed a sigh of relief. The man was back inside his saloon and enough time had elapsed for Willard to reach the gunsmith's store. He would be on his way back now.

"No I haven't! Hear me out! Like Randy Leech told you all, I'm givin' you one last chance! I want those with guns to toss them out onto the street! Then I want to see Edge and the Clayton kid leave the restaurant, go across to the wagon, climb aboard and ride away from Freedom!"

"The hell with that!" Cochran snarled, and gained a few more valuable seconds.

"Listen, Goddamnit!" Billings roared. "And save some life instead of takin' it! They do that, I give my word they'll have safe passage out of town! And I also give my word there'll be no recriminations against any citizen of Freedom for what's happened here! The world's a better place without Wilkes is my view! But I lost Grogan and Sam Jordan—you killed Sam, Cochran! But you people that are against me lost Huey Gould and I'm ready to call that quits!"

"Shit on your word, Billin's."

Sheep had started to bleat. But it was a familiar enough sound in Freedom, so that people tended not to hear the animal noise.

"I've already proved it's good!" the one-eyed man flung back at Cochran. "I could have had Edge gunned down when he came into my place. And the kid would have been as easy to kill as swatting a fly! But I gave my word they had until stage time! And I kept it!"

The cries of the sheep were louder than usual, except at shearing time when the flocks to the south of town were driven through the streets to the sheds of the large farm houses beyond the northern extent of Freedom.

"And if they don't do what you want?" Jonas Cochran called.

"Then we pour everythin' we got at your place and at the restaurant! And any of you people that are left alive will stand trial for murderin' Barny Grogan and Sam Jordan and Chris Wilkes! And you'll hang from gallows I'll have set up on the roof of the Four—"

He broke off as he realized he had to shout progressively louder to make himself heard, and suddenly became aware of the reason for this. The melancholy bleating of a vast number of sheep which were converging on the intersection from the streets to either side of the hotel.

"What the friggin' hell is goin' on?" he shrieked. Just as his uncovered eye provided him with visual proof of what his ears had already recorded. For the leading ewes trotted out onto the intersection. To be followed by countless more.

"Sheep!" Leech roared. "Bastard sheep!"

"It's a trick, Abi!" Rose Pride yelled.

"Sure pulled the wool over your eyes," Edge rasped, and rose from his hands and knees.

He was in the middle of First Street, opposite the side of the Four Aces. Ahead of him and to the right, Art Ely came erect. Two or three yards behind him, on his left, Ramon Alvarez showed himself.

On the street which ran past the other side of the hotel, Willard Clayton and Sherman Hayes emerged from among the bleating sheep.

All five of them were breathless and aching from the effort of crawling along the street in the midst of the rancid smelling animals. And they suffered more bruises from falling to the ground and being kicked by cloven hooves as they fought their way through

126

the panicking animals to the sides of the Four Aces. The sheep frightened by these abrupt flurries of activity from the men they had come to accept—then terrified by a burst of gunfire.

The shotgun in the hands of Jonas Cochran sounded first, the loads from both barrels spreading out across the intersection. Another hotel window was shattered and a number of sheep dropped to the ground, areas of their dirty white fleeces turning red.

Then Abbie Clayton fired the Tranter through the restaurant window.

Clayton tossed aside the empty shotgun and started to trigger and work the action of his repeater.

Martha Emmons ran into the restaurant and added the fire power of the Remington to the barrage of shots which rained against the front of the hotel.

The five men who had flanked the Four Aces under cover of the sheep reached side windows of the building. And saw the effect which the gunfire was having on the people inside.

Leech, Lee, Travis and the three drifters were flat to the wall beside or crouched beneath windows. Each with a cocked Winchester held ready to fire out of the windows as soon as the fusillade ended. Each face expressed a grim determination to give as good as he was taking, the moment the opportunity occurred.

Billings stood to one side of the batwings, his hands and his lower lip trembling; a grimace of flinching terror cutting deeper lines into his face as each gunshot cracked.

On the other side of the door, the booted feet of the dead Sam Jordan protruded from beneath the blanket which had been slung over his corpse. The blanket was stained crimson in a number of places.

The two bartenders could not be seen.

Some of the whores huddled on the stairway were shoved roughly to the side as Rose Pride raced up the treads.

All this seen in a moment. Before the barrel of a much-used Winchester rifle and four brand-new revolvers were smashed through panes of glass. And the five triggers were squeezed.

"No!" Billings shrieked, his plea sounding in unison with the fresh burst of gunfire. Which sent lead cracking across his once immaculate barroom—its walls now pock-marked with bullet holes, its floor spread with shards of broken glass, its atmosphere heavy with the stench of gunsmoke.

Edge's bullet took Randy Leech in the center of the man's forehead. It made a small entry hole, but burst out of his skull at the back with a more spectacular effect. So that his corpse as it slid down the wall left a broad stain of bright red.

Ely shot one of the drifters in the leg and the man came upright in reaction to the wound. And a bullet from outside gained entry through a broken window and penetrated his back to lodge in his heart.

Hayes's shot hit Travis, going in through the shoulder on a downward trajectory that directed it into his heart.

Willard and Ramon were off any mark.

"Don't kill Billin's!" the kid yelled. "I want to do—"

Lee triggered a shot from his rifle and Art Ely was flung back from a window, droplets of bright crimson spraying away from his silver hair as he fell among the milling sheep.

The twin muzzles of a double barrel shotgun showed above one end of the bar and a black face appeared beside it. The Negro drew a bead on the excited face of the shrieking Willard Clayton.

Both Edge and Ramon fired at the same target and the two bullets tunneled into flesh, shattered bone and tossed the corpse of the bartender six feet beyond the point where he died.

At the same time, the boy and Sherman Hayes loosed two bullets, firing blindly as they ducked from sight—away from shots exploded by the drifters.

Hayes was not fast enough and cried out as a bullet gouged a furrow across the side of his head. Lee's yell grew louder, as he was hit in the shoulder and spun into a half-turn, the Winchester slipping from his hands.

"Enough!" Billings screamed, and thrust his trembling hands high into the air. "We'll be slaughtered!"

"We have won!" Ramon blurted gleefully, and withdrew his gun from the window.

Hayes, with a hand pressed to the bloodied side of his head, and the excited Willard, looked tentatively in through the broken windows on the other side of the wrecked body-littered barroom. They, too, no longer aimed revolvers through the drifting gunsmoke.

Edge kept the Winchester leveled from his hip. Covering nobody, but ready at any moment to swing it to left or right—if either the men who were close to the front wall, the whores huddled on the stairway or the surviving Negro behind the bar should ignore Billings's order.

His eyes moved constantly in their slit sockets. As Billings, Lee, the two drifters and the whores stared at him. All of them aware that the lean faced man with ice chips for eyes was the decider of their fate.

"Drop those guns, you men!" Sherman Hayes demanded.

The two drifters looked from the Winchesters in their hands to the sweat-run face of Billings. As the injured veterinarian, Willard and Ramon brought their revolvers into view at the windows.

"Do it!" Billings ordered, his voice croaking.

"We got them, Cochran!" Hayes yelled as the pair of Winchesters clattered noisily to the floor.

"I am—"

Edge's rifle and the handguns of Hayes, Willard and Ramon swung toward the bar. Toward the sound of a voice and then the head of the second bartender.

"—here," the hapless Negro managed to finish in a quaking voice.

129

Before Billings shrieked, "Watch out!"

Four gun muzzles swept away from the terrified black man. To draw a bead on the crouching form of Lee. It was his left shoulder which had taken a bullet, the wound pouring blood to soak his sleeve. So he was able to draw the Colt from his holster with his right and take aim at Edge. Hatred shone through pain as he squeezed the trigger.

Jonas Cochran crashed through the batwing doors and whirled, the dead Huey Gould's shotgun leveled from his hip. And he squeezed both triggers at the same instant as Willard, Hayes, Ramon and Edge fired their guns.

The half-breed's bullet went wide and a curse ripped from between his clenched teeth as Lee's shot struck the rifle barrel to wrench it off target.

Lee did not get to see this. For three bright crimson stains suddenly encircled black holes in his chest. At the same time as his head was blasted into shreds of flesh and fragments of bone. And his decapitated corpse was flung across the body of Travis.

Silence came, with a seemingly palpable presence, into the barroom of the Four Aces.

Outside, sheep bleated.

"You won't get no trouble from us," one of the whores on the stairway rasped.

The others made mumbling sounds of agreement.

Jonas Cochran's ugly face was split by a grin that expanded to a laugh. Willard Clayton, Sherman Hayes and Ramon Alvarez smiled in relief and triumph.

"Great plan you dreamed up, mister," the owner of the Sheepman congratulated.

One of the two drifters who had been unable to tear his horrified eyes away from the bloody pulp which was all that was left of Lee's head, suddenly retched, fell to his hands and knees and vomited.

"Seems that feller figures the plot sickens," Edge drawled.

Cochran's expression saddened. "Shame about Art Ely. I seen him get hit."

"Art?" Hayes croaked, suddenly aware that the blacksmith's face was no longer at a window across the barroom.

"He was a fine *hombre*," Ramon said mournfully.

"You sure he's dead?" Hayes demanded.

Both Edge and Ramon shifted their gaze away from the interior of the barroom to look out on the street. The sheep had scattered now, sufficiently for the inert form of Ely to be seen, sprawled on the hard-packed dirt among the aimlessly wandering ewes. There was a hole in his head and blood filled his open mouth.

"*Sí, señor*," Ramon reported. "Nothing is surer than that."

"Edge?" Hayes insisted on confirmation.

The half-breed spat to one side. "Died in the wool, feller."

Chapter Fourteen

"PICK UP the gun belt and put it on, mister!" Willard Clayton ordered, his youthful features set in a hard expression of grim resolve.

"Why, for God's sake?" the one-eyed Billings pleaded, his voice still croaky with fear as he clenched his fists at his side to keep his hands from shaking.

They stood, facing each other, thirty feet apart, in front of the Four Aces Hotel. Billings with his back to the law office and the boy's back to the restaurant.

The sheep were gone now from the center of Freedom. The living animals making their own way back to the grazing meadows, while Sherman Hayes and Ramon dragged the carcasses of the dead ones off the intersection. As Edge and Jonas Cochran carried the body of Art Ely into the hotel, where it was draped by the Widow Emmons and Abbie Clayton with a linen sheet—like the bodies of Lee, Travis, one of the bartenders and one of the drifters, which had been left where they fell.

No one asked if the town undertaker should be brought to the Four Aces and nobody volunteered to go and fetch him. And, like the rest of the citizens of Freedom not directly involved in the recently fought gunbattle, the mortician himself chose to remain behind a locked door.

For, as the sun inched toward its midday zenith, those who were unable to witness what was happening in and around the hotel sensed that the killing was not yet over. For the hot air of late morning smelled of gunsmoke, sheep droppings, fresh death and impending doom.

Few words were spoken. Just two voices were raised in a sharp exchange.

"Get out here on the street, Billin's!"

"Why, boy? Why do you want to kill me?"

"Get out here, I said!"

Edge heard the shouts of the kid and the one-eyed man while he was in Ramon's bakehouse, using his razor to cut the ropes which tied the bearded Bart Briggs to the big table.

"What's happenin'?" the frightened stage driver asked.

"None of our business, feller," the half-breed told him. "Go get your rig ready to roll, uh?"

Briggs scurried out ahead of Edge, went to the door of the stage-line depot and banged a fist on it. "You got some mail and freight to go, Jake?" he asked, looking back over his shoulder toward the hotel and the two figures standing in front of it.

Edge hoisted his saddle and bedroll from the sidewalk and tossed it onto the railed roof of the stage. Then leaned against a rear wheel of the rig and took out the makings from a pocket of his shirt.

"Gray mare down in Ely's livery," he said to Sherman Hayes, who sat in the rocker on the sidewalk out front of the restaurant, allowing Martha Emmons to bathe the bullet wound in his right temple.

"Yours?" the veterinarian asked, unable to shift his gaze from Billings and Clayton.

"Yeah. Thrush in two hooves. Obliged if you'd take care of it. Or shoot the animal if it's gone too far."

"Be happy to."

Now Edge looked toward the main point of interest in Freedom. As did the Widow Emmons. Their attention captured by Willard's demand that Billings should arm himself, and the response of the one-eyed man.

The gunbelt to which the boy referred belonged to one of the surviving drifters who, with his partner and the Negro bartender stood on the hotel stoop, apprehensive under the threat of the double-barrel shotgun Jonas Cochran aimed at them. Ramon Alvarez had unbuckled the belt from the man's waist, pushed his gun into the holster and tossed it so that it fell in front of Billings's booted feet.

The whores and Rose Pride—her face bruised and crusted with dried blood from the beating the one-eyed man had given her—looked down on the scene from the upper rooms of the hotel.

"You called yourself Smith many years ago," Abbie Clayton replied to Billings's pleading question. "In St. Louis. Where you shot a man who caught you cheating at cards. Man you murdered was named Clayton."

The beautiful blue-eyed blond with the statuesque body stood in the doorway of the law office.

Billings wrenched his gaze away from the boy to look hard into the equally resolute face of his sister. He looked too long and too hard—obviously trying to recognize Abbie as she might have looked fifteen years earlier. So that when he started to say, "I'm afraid you must be mistaken," there was no one who saw and heard him who believed he was telling the truth.

"It was our Pa you shot down, mister!" Willard rasped.

"You are brother and sister?" Billings was genuinely surprised.

"Our Pa didn't have a gun when you killed him," the boy went on, as if he had not even heard the words of the one-eyed man. "But I'm ready to give you a better chance than he had. Because I'm not the kinda killer you are, Billin's. Now, pick up that damn gunbelt!"

135

A brief silence clamped over the town again. Broken when Edge struck a match on a wheelrim of the stage. Then the one-eyed man unclenched his fists, and broke out in a new sweat as his fingers trembled.

"Very well," he said, and dropped slowly into a crouch.

Willard turned slightly, splayed his feet wider and bent his left hand so that it was level with the butt of the Tranter jutting from his belly holster.

"Be careful, Willard!" Abbie warned. "He cheats at cards."

Billings's hand became rock-steady as he picked up the gunbelt, slung it around his waist, fastened the buckle and straightened. There was still sweat on his face and wet stains on his shirt from his armpits. But he was no longer in the grip of fear. He stood in a casual attitude, muscles relaxed and expression revealing nothing of what he felt. Not in the gunfighter's pose which the boy had so awkwardly adopted, but looking as if he could take it up in part of a second.

"Yes, son, be very careful," he said, in his Southern lazy drawl. "I've got some kind of vague recollection that I shot and killed a card cheat in St. Louis a lot of years ago."

The Claytons' tension mounted and the boy moved his hand fractionally nearer the butt of the Tranter as his sister made to speak, but held back as Billings continued.

"And I might well have called myself Smith. Called myself all kinds of different names all the time. But one thing I've never done is gunned down an unarmed man."

"You—" Willard started.

"Shut up and listen, son," Billings interrupted flatly. "You gave me a chance, so I'm giving you one. I never had to shoot down an unarmed man because it was never necessary. Because at the time you're talking about, I was one of the fastest guns around. Which is why I used all kinds of different

136

names. Because, like now, I didn't like killing men way back when."

Edge drew deeply against his cigarette and recalled something the one-eyed man had said in the Four Aces earlier, *"The gun's not my way anymore."*

"You ain't scarin' me!" Willard flung at Billings, and both his voice and expression gave the lie to his words.

"You're scarin' the hell out of me, son," Billings went on in the same easy tone of voice. "Because I don't want to have to kill you. This gunbelt you made me put on is the first I've worn in ten years. But I haven't forgotten how to use a six-shooter, son. Which is why I give you fair warning. That if you draw against me, I'll kill you. Though I don't want to. Because it'll be a waste of your life. I never cheated at cards. Because I was as good with them as with a gun. Your sister was younger then than you are now. She was told lies and believed them."

"No," Abbie cried.

It was as if Billings had never heard her. And he began to talk not just to Willard Clayton now. He started to address everyone in Freedom but, knowing the futility of any more attempts to win them over, he did not raise his voice.

"When I won enough in a game to build the Four Aces, I decided to turn my back on cards and the gun. Become a businessman. And operate as straight as I did in the old days. And I could have done well for myself here. Well for the town as well. But it wasn't meant to be, I guess."

He became pensive as he spoke the final words and he raised one ringed hand toward his face, the index finger aimed at his nose.

Willard went for his gun.

"No!" Abbie shrieked.

"Abi!" Rose Pride yelled from the second story window of the hotel.

A gunshot cracked. To put a full stop to a series of actions that merged into a single fluid movement of

137

Billings's right hand. Which resulted in Willard Clayton taking a bullet in his heart even before the muzzle of his uncocked Tranter was clear of the holster.

"Who—?" Martha Emmons gasped through the hands she had flung to her face.

Willard took a backward step, gazed down in surprise at the bloodstain on his shirt front, and then fell into a heap in front of the sidewalk.

"The kid," Edge said through a cloud of blue cigarette smoke.

"No more!" Sherman Hayes roared, powering to his feet from the rocker as Cochran swung the shotgun toward Billings. "Freedom's had its fill of killing."

Abbie flung herself down into a crouch beside her dead brother.

The one-eyed man thrust his still smoking revolver into the holster, unfastened the buckle and let the belt drop around his ankles.

The clock in the dry-goods store began to chime the hour of noon.

Some people thought they could see the shadows begin to lengthen again.

Abbie Clayton clawed a hand toward the Tranter which had fallen from Willard's grasp and holster.

Edge drew his Remington and triggered a shot across the intersection. The bullet hit the revolver on the street and kicked it a foot beyond the woman's reaching fingers.

"Billings has no reason to lie, lady!" the half-breed said as all eyes swung away from the gun in the dust to stare at Edge.

The woman sobbed.

The half-breed slid his revolver into the holster.

"Sherman Hayes is right," the saloon keeper agreed and allowed the shotgun barrels to tilt toward the ground. "Same as the stranger is. But we don't want Billin's nor any of his people here in town."

"It is my intention to leave, sir," the unlikely looking former gunslinger said, shifting his one-eyed gaze from Edge to the bald-headed owner of the Sheepman. "And in time Freedom could discover it's the town's loss."

"Can we come, Abi?" the redheaded whore called down eagerly.

"Anyone who wants to is welcome," Billings invited, raking his eyes over the windows with the whores at them and then the Negro bartender and the two drifters.

"Me, too?" Rose Pride wanted to know nervously.

Billings smiled. "Sure, darling. We'll go someplace where our kind of business will be welcomed."

The madam's bruised and cut face was abruptly wreathed with a smile. "That place we was goin' to first? The town south of here those Mormon people abandoned?"

Billings flicked his fingers. "Why not? There's no one there any more. No one to stand in our way of making it the most wide-open Goddamn town in the US of A." His smile was a match for that of Rose Pride. "Sure, sweetheart! We'll go to Las Vegas!"

As he went up the steps of the hotel, Jonas Cochran moved out of his way.

Ramon started across the intersection toward his restaurant while Martha Emmons hurried over to where Abbie Clayton kneeled beside her dead brother, sobbing.

"Where are you going, Mr. Edge?" Sherman Hayes asked, dropping back into the rocker and exploring his injury with careful fingers. As the half-breed pulled open the nearside door of the stage.

"No place, feller."

"But you're leaving."

"All I ever do. Never do get any place."

He dropped into a seat, his back to the way the stage was headed. And allowed a column of smoke to rise in front of his face from the cigarette angled out of the corner of his mouth.

"It wasn't all for nothing, you know," the veterinarian said morosely. "It might seem that way now,

139

but this town's going to be a better place to live in after Billings and his bunch are gone."

Hayes peered along Main Street beyond the stage and then swung his gaze in other directions to look along the two streets which flanked the Four Aces. To where the townspeople of Freedom who had taken no part in the gun-battle were beginning to emerge nervously from behind the safety of walls, unmarked by bullet holes and not stained by blood.

"Si señor," Ramon Alvarez agreed eagerly. "The town is saved. You, *Señor* Edge. The *Señors* Hayes and Jonas Cochran. The poor dead boy and *Señor* Ely. And me. One day, all will be agreed that we six were magnificent!"

The half-breed took the cigarette from his mouth and ground it out under his boot heel as the stage tilted and creaked with the weight of Bart Briggs. Then, as he touched the brim of his hat before tipping it forward over his bristled face, he answered; "I guess we did all right. But you can bet your ass some wise guy'll come along and go one better."

Dear Reader:

The Pinnacle Books editors strive to select and produce books that are exciting, entertaining and readable . . . no matter what the category. From time to time we will attempt to discover what you, the reader, think about a particular book or series.

Now that you've finished reading this volume in the *Edge* series, we'd like to find out what you liked, or didn't like, about this story. We'll share your opinions with the author and discuss them as we plan future books. This will result in books that you will find more to your liking. As in fine art and good cooking, a matter of taste is involved; and for you, of course, it is *your* taste that is most important to you. For George G. Gilman and the Pinnacle editors, it is not the critics' reviews and publicity that have been most rewarding, it is the unending stream of readers' mail. Here is where we discover what readers like, what they *feel* about a story, and what they find memorable. So, do help us in becoming a little more knowledgeable in providing you with the kind of stories you like. Here's how . . .

WIN BOOKS . . . AND $200! Please fill out the following pages and mail them as indicated. Every week, for twelve weeks following publication, the editors will choose, at random, a reader's name from all the questionnaires received. The twelve lucky readers will receive $25 worth of paperbacks *and* become official entrants in our Pinnacle Books Reader Sweepstakes. The winner of this sweepstakes drawing will receive a Grand Prize of $200, the inclusion of his or her name in a forthcoming Pinnacle Book (as a special acknowledgment, possibly even as a character!), and several other local prizes to be announced to each initial winner. As a further inducement to send in your questionnaire *now,* we will also send the first 25 replies received a free book by return mail! Here's a chance to talk to the author and editors, voice your opinions, and win some great prizes, too!

—The Editors

READER SURVEY

NOTE: Please feel free to expand on any of these questions on a separate page, or to express yourself on any aspect of your thoughts on reading . . . but do be sure to include this entire questionnaire with any such letters.

1. Are you glad you bought this book, and did it live up to your expectations? _____

2. What was it about this book that induced you to buy it?

   (A. The title_____) (B. The author's name_____)
   (C. A friend's recommendation_____)
   (D. The cover art_____)
   (E. The cover description_____)
   (F. Subject matter_____) (G. Advertisement_____)
   (H. Heard author on TV or radio_____)
   (I. Read previous books in this series_____ . . . which ones? _____)
   (J. Bookstore display_____)
   (K. Other? _____)

3. What is the book you read just before this one?

   And how would you rate it with this volume in the *Edge* series? _____

4. What is the very next book you plan to read?

   How did you decide on that? _____

5. Where did you buy this volume in the *Edge* series? _____

(Name and address of store, please):

_____

_____

6. Where do you buy the majority of your paper-backs? _____

7. What seems to be the major factor that persuades you to buy a certain book? _____
_____

8. How many books do you buy each month?
_____

9. Do you ever write letters to the author or pub-lisher . . . and why? _____
_____

10. About how many hours a week do you spend reading books? ____ How many hours a week watching television? ____

11. What other spare-time activity do you enjoy most?
_____ For how many hours a week? ____

12. Which magazines do you read regularly? . . . in order of your preference _____,
_____, _____,
_____, _____

13. Of your favorite magazine, what is it that you like best about it? _____
_____

14. What is your favorite television show of the past year or so? _____

15. What is your favorite motion picture of the past year or so? _____

16. What is the most disappointing television show you've seen lately? _____

17. What is the most disappointing motion picture you've seen lately? _____

18. What is the most disappointing book you've read lately? _____

19. Are there authors that you like so well that you read *all* their books? _____
    Who are they? _____

20. And can you explain *why* you like their books so much? _____
    _____
    _____

21. Which particular books by these authors do you like best? _____

22. Did you read Taylor Caldwell's *Captains and the Kings*? _____ Did you watch it on TV? _____
    Which did you do first? _____

23. Did you read John Jakes' *The Bastard*? _____
    Did you watch it on TV? _____ Which first? _____
    Have you read any of the other books in John Jakes' Bicentennial Series? _____
    What do you think of them? _____

24. Did you read James Michener's *Centennial*? _____
    Did you watch it on TV? _____ Which first? _____

25. Did you read Irwin Shaw's *Rich Man, Poor Man*? _____ Did you watch it on TV? _____ Which first? _____

26. Of all the recent books you've read, or films you've seen, are there any that you would compare in any way to *Edge*? _____

27. With series books that you like, how often would you like to read them . . . (a) twice a year _____? (b) three times a year _____? (c) every other month _____? (d) every month _____? (e) other _____?

28. What is your favorite book character or series of all time? _____ And why? _____

29. Do you collect any paperback series? _____ Which ones? _____

30. What do you like *best* about the *Edge* series? _____

31. And what don't you like about it . . . if anything? _____

32. Have you read any books in *The Destroyer* series? _____ And what is your opinion of them? _____

33. Have you read any books in the Nick Carter *Killmaster* series? _____ Opinion? _____

34. Have you read any books in the *Apache* series? _____ Opinion? _____

35. Have you read any books in *The Penetrator* series? _____ Opinion? _____
_____

36. Have you read any books in the *Steele* series? _____ Opinion? _____
_____

37. Have you read any books in the *Zane Grey* series? _____ Opinion? _____
_____

38. Have you read any books in the *Louis L'Amour* western series? _____ Opinion? _____
_____

39. Have you read any books in the *Lone Ranger* series? _____ Opinion? _____
_____

40. Have you read any books in the *Jake Logan* series? _____ Opinion? _____
_____

41. Have you read any books in the *Max Brand* series? _____ Opinion? _____
_____

42. Rank the following descriptions of the *Edge* series as you feel they are best defined:

	Excellent	Okay	Poor
A. A sense of reality	_____	_____	_____
B. Suspense	_____	_____	_____
C. Intrigue	_____	_____	_____
D. Sexuality	_____	_____	_____
E. Violence	_____	_____	_____

F. Romance   _____ _____ _____

G. History   _____ _____ _____

H. Characterization   _____ _____ _____

I. Scenes, events   _____ _____ _____

J. Pace, readability   _____ _____ _____

K. Dialogue   _____ _____ _____

L. Style   _____ _____ _____

43. What do you do with your paperbacks after you've read them? _____
_____

44. Do you buy paperbacks in any of the following categories, and approximately how many do you buy in a year?

A. Contemporary fiction   _____

B. Historical romance   _____

C. Family saga   _____

D. Romance (like Harlequin)   _____

E. Romantic suspense   _____

F. Gothic romance   _____

G. Occult novels   _____

H. War novels   _____

I. Action/adventure novels   _____

J. "Bestsellers"   _____

K. Science fiction   _____

L. Mystery   _____

M. Westerns   _____

N. Nonfiction   ——

O. Biography   ——

P. How-To books   ——

Q. Other _____

45. And, lastly, some profile data on *you* the reader . . .

    A. Age: 12–16____ 17–20____ 21–30____
        31–40____ 41–50____ 51–60____
        61 or over____

    B. Occupation: _____
    _____

    C. Education level; check last grade completed:
    10 ____ 11 ____ 12 ____ Freshman ____
    Sophomore ____ Junior ____ Senior ____
    Graduate School ____, plus any specialized
    schooling _____

    D. Your average annual gross income:
    Under $10,000____ $10,000–$15,000____
    $15,000–$20,000____ $20,000–$30,000____
    $30,000–$50,000____ Above $50,000____

    E. Did you read a lot as a child? ____ Do you
    recall your favorite childhood novel? ____
    _____

    F. Do you find yourself reading more or less
    than you did five years ago? ____

    G. Do you read hardcover books? ____ How
    often? ____ If so, are they books that you
    buy? ____ borrow? ____ or trade? ____ Or
    other? ____

H. Does the imprint (Pinnacle, Avon, Bantam, etc.) make any difference to you when considering a paperback purchase? _____

I. Have you ever bought paperbacks by mail directly from the publisher? _____ And do you like to buy books that way? _____

J. Would you be interested in buying paperbacks via a book club or subscription program? _____ And, in your opinion, what would be the best reasons for doing so? _____ _____ . . . the problems in doing so? _____

K. Is there something that you'd like to see writers or publishers do for you as a reader of paperbacks? _____
_____

L. Would you be interested in joining an *Edge* fan club? _____

M. If so, which of the following items would interest you most:

	GREAT IDEA!	DEPENDS . . .	FORGET IT!
Monthly Newsletter	_____	_____	_____
Membership card	_____	_____	_____
Membership scroll (for framing)	_____	_____	_____
T-shirt	_____	_____	_____
Sweat shirt	_____	_____	_____
Windbreaker jacket	_____	_____	_____
Poster	_____	_____	_____
Decal	_____	_____	_____
Other ideas?	_____		

(On those items above that you *do* like, indicate what you think a fair price would be.)

*THANK YOU FOR TAKING THE TIME TO RE-
PLY TO THIS, THE FIRST PUBLIC READER
SURVEY IN PAPERBACK HISTORY!*

NAME _____

ADDRESS _____

CITY_____ **STATE**_____ **ZIP**_____

PHONE _____

Please return this questionnaire to:

**The Editors; Survey Dept. EDS
Pinnacle Books, Inc.
2029 Century Park East
Los Angeles, CA 90067**

Subject to all federal, state, and local restrictions; void
where prohibited by law.

EDGE BY George G. Gilman

Josiah Hedges is no ordinary man — he's a violent gunslinger.
Created out of fury, hardened by death and destruction, he's
rough, but not as rough as the fate of those who get in his way.

Over 4 million copies in print!

☐ 40-504-9	Loner	#1	$1.50
☐ 40-505-7	Ten Grand	#2	1.50
☐ 40-506-5	Apache Death	#3	1.50
☐ 40-484-0	Killer's Breed	#4	1.50
☐ 40-507-3	Blood On Silver	#5	1.50
☐ 40-536-7	Red River	#6	1.50
☐ 40-461-1	California Kill	#7	1.50
☐ 40-580-4	Hell's Seven	#8	1.50
☐ 40-581-2	Bloody Summer	#9	1.50
☐ 40-430-1	Black Vengeance	#10	1.50
☐ 40-582-0	Sioux Uprising	#11	1.50
☐ 40-583-9	Death's Bounty	#12	1.50
☐ 40-462-X	Hated	#13	1.50
☐ 40-537-5	Tiger's Gold	#14	1.50
☐ 40-407-7	Paradise Loses	#15	1.50
☐ 40-431-X	Final Shot	#16	1.50
☐ 40-584-7	Vengeance Valley	#17	1.50
☐ 40-538-3	Ten Tombstones	#18	1.50
☐ 40-539-1	Ashes and Dust	#19	1.50
☐ 40-541-3	Sullivan's Law	#20	1.50
☐ 40-585-5	Rhapsody in Red	#21	1.50
☐ 40-487-5	Slaughter Road	#22	1.50
☐ 40-485-9	Echoes of War	#23	1.50
☐ 40-486-7	Slaughterday	#24	1.50
☐ 40-488-3	Violence Trail	#25	1.50
☐ 40-579-0	Savage Dawn	#26	1.50
☐ 40-203-1	Death Drive	#27	1.50
☐ 40-204-X	Eve of Evil	#28	1.50
☐ 40-502-2	The Living, the Dying and the Dead	#29	1.50

PINNACLE-BOOK MAILING SERVICE
P.O. Box 690, New York, NY 10019

Please send me the books I have checked above. Enclosed is my check
or money order for $_____.(Please add 50¢ per order and 10¢ per book
to cover postage and handling. New York State and California residents
add applicable sales tax.) Please allow approximately four weeks for delivery.

Name_____

Address_____

City_____ State/Zip_____

From America's
#1 series publisher,

by William M. James

He is Cuchillo Oro—Apache for Golden Knife. Fighting a one-man battle against the invading white man, he is not afraid to kill or to be killed. And now, there is no turning back—not for Cuchillo, and not for those who have persecuted his people!

Over 625,000 copies in print!

☐	40-550-2	The First Death	#1	$1.50
☐	40-551-0	Knife in the Night	#2	1.50
☐	40-552-9	Duel to the Death	#3	1.50
☐	40-553-7	The Death Train	#4	1.50
☐	40-554-5	Fort Treachery	#5	1.50
☐	40-555-3	Sonora Slaughter	#6	1.50
☐	40-556-1	Blood Line	#7	1.50
☐	40-557-X	Blood on the Tracks	#8	1.50
☐	40-558-8	The Naked and the Savage	#9	1.50
☐	40-559-6	All Blood is Red	#10	1.50
☐	50-560-X	The Cruel Trail	#11	1.50
☐	40-355-0	Fools Gold	#12	1.50
☐	40-356-9	Best Man	#13	1.50

PINNACLE-BOOK MAILING SERVICE
P.O. Box 690, New York, NY 10019

Please send me the books I have checked above. Enclosed is my check or money order for $_____. (Please add 50¢ per order and 10¢ per book to cover postage and handling. New York State and California residents add applicable sales tax.)

Name_____

Address_____

City_____ State/Zip_____
Please allow approximately four weeks for delivery.